*Books by Margaret Mounsdon
in the Linford Romance Library:*

FINN'S FOREST

When her son Gareth wins a competition for a stay in Finn's Forest, Eirlys Pendragon is at first thrilled, and charmed by its owner, Finn Hart. But it's anything but plain sailing as the manicured and tactless Miranda, wife of the camp's wealthy financier, takes an instant dislike to Eirlys, and her bullying son singles out Gareth. Eirlys believes the only way to deal with fear is to face up to it — but flying down a zip wire into Finn's arms seems an extreme solution to the problem . . .

MARGARET MOUNSDON

♦

FINN'S
FOREST

Complete and Unabridged

LINFORD
Leicester

First published in Great Britain in 2015

First Linford Edition
published 2016

C463803283

A catalogue record for this book is available
from the British Library.

ISBN 978–1–4448–2839–9

Published by
F. A. Thorpe (Publishing)
Anstey, Leicestershire

Set by Words & Graphics Ltd.
Anstey, Leicestershire
Printed and bound in Great Britain by
T. J. International Ltd., Padstow, Cornwall

This book is printed on acid-free paper

1

'I'm so sorry. I thought this was the office.'

Covered in confusion, Eirlys started to back out of the room. It wasn't easy, what with Gareth doing his best to poke his head round his mother's legs to find out what was going on. 'Who's that lady?' he demanded loudly. 'And why's she kissing the man? Are they playing postman's knock?'

'What are you doing snooping around here?' The woman showed no sign of embarrassment, despite the compromising situation. The man she had been embracing moved away from her, the expression on his weathered face unreadable.

Eirlys stopped backing out of the room. 'I was not snooping.' She was not in the wrong here, and if this woman wanted a confrontation Eirlys was in the right mood. It was a hot day. She and Gareth had endured a long journey in an over-crowded coach full of excited children on their half-term break, who had been overjoyed when the ancient vehicle had broken down. Not so overjoyed by this development themselves, Eirlys and Gareth had sat on the grass verge while the hoses under the bonnet steamed and the driver scratched his head and waited for the emergency services to deal with the situation. It had taken another two hours for a replacement vehicle to arrive, by which time Gareth was thirsty, tired and whining.

To give the coach company their due, the new driver on the job was the young managing director, full of profuse apologies, bottles of water to quench their thirst, and offers of refunds or a complimentary trip sometime in the future to a destination of their choice. After that everyone cheered up, and with the recommencement of the journey the passengers were soon in a better frame of mind; but the incident had significantly delayed

Eirlys' arrival and she was not about to be picked on by a woman who, from the expression on her face, clearly thought Eirlys and her son had crawled out from under a stone.

'We've come to check in,' she explained, glancing at the casually dressed man who was now busy checking a chart. 'I'm Eirlys Pendragon and this is my son Gareth.'

'You're over two hours late,' the man spoke for the first time. Eirlys rather liked the Welsh lilt to his voice, and if the situation hadn't been so tense she might have liked him too.

'And you are — ?' Eirlys flashed her eyes at him. One more word of censure from either of them and she and Gareth were out of here, competition prize or not.

'Miranda Hargreaves,' the woman drawled, although the question had not been directed at her.

A reluctant smile curved the man's lips. 'I'm sorry; I should have introduced myself. It's been a busy day.'

'So I see.' Eirlys glanced at the blonde woman.

'Finn Hart. Welcome to Finn's Forest.'

'Yes, well, Mr Hart . . . ' she began.

'It's Finn,' he interrupted.

'We've had a busy day too,' a slightly mollified Eirlys replied. 'I apologise for being late but it was due to circumstances outside our control.'

An uneasy silence followed while they all took stock of the situation.

Finn broke the silence and solemnly shook the little boy's hand. 'This, I presume, is Gareth?'

'The bus broke down,' Gareth explained, 'and the police came and talked to us, and I saw the radios in their car, and one of them let me try his hat on. It wasn't a helmet.' He looked disappointed. 'Only a flat cap. But it had a badge, and he showed me his special number on his shirt.'

'After all that excitement you must be hungry,' Finn replied.

Miranda, who had been playing with a pile of paperclips, wrinkled her nose.

4

'I would suggest a quick shower first might be in order.'

Eirlys was wearing a crumpled summer dress that had been clean on that morning, but Gareth had spilled juice down it, and with the heat of the sun and the long hours since she had combed her hair she knew neither she nor Gareth were looking their best.

'We could do with freshening up,' Eirlys admitted; then in an attempt to defuse the situation, added, 'Although the pair of us look like hobos, we're quite respectable really.'

'There is some paperwork to be completed,' Finn replied with a sympathetic smile, 'but nothing that can't wait until the morning. I'll get one of the rangers to show you to your cabins.'

'There's more than one?' Eirlys asked. 'Cabin, I mean.'

'The boys share. There is separate accommodation for visitors.'

'I'm not a visitor. I'm staying too,' Eirlys insisted. 'Couldn't Gareth and I share?'

'You are classed as a visitor,' Finn replied equally firmly. 'I'm sure you don't want your son to feel different from the other boys, do you?'

'He already is,' a voice broke into the exchange.

'Sorry?' Eirlys had almost forgotten the other woman was still in the room.

'Different. Finn tells me your son goes to a village school and that you live in a caravan. How novel.'

'My private life is none of your affair.' Eirlys turned on Finn. 'How dare you discuss my personal details with anyone else?'

'Miranda does the publicity for the camp,' Finn explained. 'When your name was announced as our competition winner, she offered to do a piece for the local newspaper. I thought it might be a good idea, but only with your approval of course.'

Eirlys' head began to spin. She was too tired to think straight. Gareth had been up early, full of excitement, and ready hours before the coach was due to leave. Neither of them had slept much the night before, and all Eirlys now wanted was a hot shower, something to eat, then her bed.

There was a tap on the door and a young girl poked her head round. 'Finn? Did you want me?'

Finn greeted the new arrival with a smile of relief. 'Dixie. Come in.'

Dixie was wearing a T-shirt overprinted with the distinctive logo of Finn's Forest, and practical cargo pants. Her hair was tied back in a neat ponytail, and her complexion boasted a healthy outdoor glow.

'This is Eirlys Pendragon and her son Gareth. They've been delayed,' Finn explained. 'But now they're here, do you think you could offer them the usual forest welcome?'

'No problem.' Dixie smiled. 'I'm Dixie Ash. Just the name for a girl working with trees,' she added, 'and I've done all the jokes.'

'Dixie's one of our rangers,' Finn explained. 'She's on duty tonight, so if you've any problems . . . ' He nodded in her direction.

'I'm your girl,' Dixie finished his sentence.

Eirlys warmed to the fresh-faced ranger. 'Thank you.'

'You must be absolutely exhausted after your journey. Everything's ready for you. Come this way.'

At long last feeling she was receiving the welcome she deserved, Eirlys picked up their backpacks.

'Let me take those,' Dixie offered.

'I can carry mine,' Gareth insisted, 'but you can help Mum if you like.'

'All right, young man, why don't we do just that?' Dixie whipped Eirlys' backpack out of her hands and in another swift movement slipped her arms through the straps. 'Wanna hold my hand?' she invited Gareth. 'That way no one will get lost.'

'Are there any bears outside?' he asked in an awed voice as he slipped a shy hand into Dixie's.

'If there are we'll fight 'em off, won't

we? You, me, and Mum.'

'Yay.' Gareth jigged up and down.

'Come on then.'

'Hurry up, Mum,' he urged as Eirlys threw Finn a less-than-friendly look.

'See you later.' He remained unruffled. Ignoring Miranda, Eirlys followed Gareth and Dixie out of the office. The trio picked their way across the compound towards the rear of the complex.

'I know things look a little basic,' Dixie replied with a sunny smile, 'but the shower block is state-of-the-art.'

'How many cabins are there?' Eirlys asked.

'There are a couple for the boys; then there are the staff quarters, the office, the cookhouse, showers, laundry, medical centre, and the visitors' accommodation. You're up in what's called the attic. It's above a storeroom I'm afraid, but it's very cosy. We'll do the grand tour in the morning.'

They came to a halt by a wooden building that boasted a row of brightly coloured pegs outside the door. 'Here we are.' Dixie unhooked two towels. 'See that number under the peg?' she asked Gareth as she pointed to the painted numerals. Gareth nodded. 'You're number six, and Eirlys is number seven. If you hang your wet towels here when you've finished with them they'll dry overnight. They get changed every other day. I should point out that everyone is also responsible for leaving things as they find them. So when you've had your shower, if you wouldn't mind making sure the soap dispenser isn't dripping and the shower is turned off properly, that would be terrific.' Dixie tempered her words with a friendly smile. 'I'm sure you would anyway, but I have to complete my tick chart and that's one of the conditions that has to be explained to you.'

Gareth looked to his mother for reassurance. 'We've got that,' Eirlys told her.

'Good. You'll find everything you need inside,' Dixie said. 'The boys' facilities are actually in a separate block through the adjoining door, but for tonight I don't think it will matter if you use the same unit. There's a curtain for privacy so you won't be disturbed. You can make one shower into two units.'

'Thank you,' Eirlys replied, relieved she wasn't going to have to tidy up two shower blocks.

'Then I'll leave you. The kitchen block is over there.' Dixie pointed across the complex. The door was ajar, creating a beam of light in the dusk, and through the gap Eirlys could see a large lady stirring a huge saucepan of something fragrant and steamy. 'Hannah will have soup ready for you when you're through, if you'd like to make your way over. You've no special dietary requirements?'

'I eat everything,' Gareth announced proudly, 'but I don't like spaghetti.'

'Me neither. It's all slippery and horrible,' Dixie agreed.

The smile Gareth bestowed on her convinced Eirlys that her son had found a friend for life.

'I'm very hungry,' Gareth said. 'We had sandwiches for lunch, but that was hours ago, and my chocolate melted in the sun so I couldn't eat it.'

'Then we'd better be as quick as we can in the shower, Gareth.' Eirlys took hold of his arm. 'Now Dixie's a busy girl, so let's leave her to get on with her duties whilst we clean ourselves up.'

'It's very big,' Gareth said in a voice full of awe as they made their way through to the showers.

Eirlys was pleased to notice it was clean and surprisingly warm inside the unit, and she had to agree with Gareth that it was indeed spacious. A part of her had been dreading cold showers in a wooden hut, but here there was a lingering aroma of pine essence and all the surfaces were spotless.

Fifteen minutes later, with squeaky-clean hair and smelling of Norwegian pine after having liberally cleansed themselves with a generous supply of shower gel, Eirlys and Gareth hung their towels as requested on the correct hooks. Eirlys was now dressed in serviceable three-quarter-length pedal pushers and T-shirt. Gareth was wearing his favourite jeans and clean T-shirt too.

'Let me show you the way to the catering unit,' a voice came at them out of nowhere.

'It's Finn, Mum. No need to jump,' Gareth chided as the silhouette emerged from the twilight.

'If you've come to check up on us,' Eirlys snapped, 'we followed Dixie's instructions to the letter. The showers are exactly as we found them and anyone wishing to use them would have no cause to complain.'

'I'm pleased to hear it,' was Finn's calm reply. 'There aren't many rules in the camp, but you'll find the ten basic ones on the wall in your room and I insist they are followed to the letter. Now who's hungry?'

'I am,' Gareth responded to the challenge.

'Good. Hannah does a mean tomato soup, and we've got beans on toast to follow.'

'Wicked.' Gareth danced up and down with excitement.

'Eirlys?'

The way Finn said her name made her fingers tingle. Convincing herself it was nothing more than her skin reacting to the stimulation of a pine-scented shower, Eirlys responded in as calm a voice as she could manage, 'That sounds lovely. Will Miranda be joining us?'

'No,' Finn replied. 'She's gone out to dinner with her husband.'

'She's married?'

'Yes. You'll probably bump into her husband Philip sometime. He's often about the place.'

Eirlys' cheeks burned in the darkness. She bit her lip. It would do no good reminding Finn that from where she'd been standing a little over an hour ago Miranda's behaviour hadn't looked to be that of a married woman. She made a mental note to have as little as possible to do with Finn Hart.

'Now I suggest we all get over to the cookhouse.' The tone of Finn's voice suggested he knew exactly what was going through Eirlys' mind.

2

Eirlys and Gareth had eaten in the kitchen block with the staff and a few hangers-on dressed in high-visibility jackets over industrial overalls.

'Hannah's such a good cook, none of the delivery men want to go home until they've had a bowl of her soup to fortify them for the journey. I'm Dean Robinson.' A cheerful young man nodded at some drivers, who raised their soup spoons in acknowledgement of his remarks before pulling out a chair for Eirlys. 'And this must be Gareth,' he said.

The child clung shyly to his mother's arm.

'Come and sit by me, Gareth,' Dixie called out; and with an alarming turn of speed, Gareth deserted his mother and raced over to join his new friend.

'You'll have to watch out, Dean,' one

of the drivers joked. 'You've got competition. Dixie's found a new boyfriend.'

Finn brought the proceedings to order, ignoring Dean's heightened colour. 'Talking of competition, some of you may not be aware, but Eirlys and Gareth are our first competition winners.'

A round of applause broke out. Dixie leaned forward in excitement. 'Tell us all about it. I've never met a competition winner before.'

'Let the poor girl eat in peace.' Hannah was busy ladling tomato soup into bowls, while her assistant cut up chunks of homemade bread and passed them round.

In between mouthfuls of the best soup Eirlys had tasted in years, she explained how she'd always loved living close to nature and that she'd seen a flyer for Finn's Forest in her local library, inviting entrants to compose a small piece of prose outlining their reasons for wanting to join a Finn's Forest party in the summer.

Gareth stifled a huge yawn as he proudly announced, 'And we won.'

Eirlys cast a regretful look at Hannah. 'I really think that we won't be able to finish our supper.'

'Don't worry about it.' The cook ruffled Gareth's hair. 'This young man looks dead on his feet. Not surprising after the day he's had. Off you go to bed, my lad.'

Dixie stood up. 'I'll escort you over to the accommodation.'

'I don't want to put anyone out,' Eirlys began.

'Dixie is night shift supervisor,' Finn said with calm authority, 'so there's no question of anyone putting her out.'

Again it was difficult for Eirlys to tell what Finn was thinking. 'Good night,' she addressed those seated round the table.

She left to cries of, 'See you in the morning.'

* * *

A bugle blast roused Eirlys from the deepest of slumbers. She moaned and

17

thrust her head under her pillow, but the noise wouldn't stop. What was going on?

She opened her reluctant eyes. The room smelt and looked different from her snug bedroom in Martha's bungalow, and the sounds coming through the open window were not those of her usual wake-up chorus when she overnighted at the caravan. There was no inquisitive robin pecking at her window or cows coughing in the morning mist. Instead she could hear the pounding of feet and lots of laughter.

She snuggled down under the duvet and watched the morning sun dance patterns on the cool cotton cover as she gathered her thoughts, remembering she was in Finn's Forest, a place the brochure described as magical. She didn't know about magical, but it was certainly different. Her life the other side of the River Severn was nothing like this.

Eirlys hadn't seen much of anything yet, but she was inclined to believe the site's publicity. She knew the settlement used to be the site of cottages inhabited by forest workers. Legend had it that they'd set up overnight, making sure smoke could be seen from their chimneys before sunset the next day. By following this rule of lore, no permission was needed to establish ownership. The land was theirs.

Eirlys could understand why they had picked such a beautiful area. The forest was steeped in history, from the days when the Romans first camped there, to Civil War battles and local skirmishes.

Over the years the settlement had fallen into disrepair. Life had changed and people moved away to look for work in the new industrialised cities. Finn Hart had recently established an activity centre for boys on the site of the old settlement. The project was in its early stages, but Finn's mission statement was to provide a unique experience for young people, and his plan was to extend the facilities if the initial project was a viable success.

With a yelp of shock Eirlys realised

the time. It was well after half past seven and breakfast was only served until half past eight. Leaping out of bed, she gave another yelp as she remembered too late Dixie's advice about not standing upright. The attic beams were so low that it was impossible for a normal adult to stand upright.

'That's why we keep the area for sleeping only,' she had explained, stooping over the plumped-up the pillows on the large double bed. 'It's very peaceful here so you shouldn't be disturbed. Sleep well.'

And Eirlys had. The room was sparsely furnished with the minimum of essentials, and she was glad she had followed Finn's advice to keep personal possessions light.

The only adornment in the room besides the emergency advice on what to do in case of fire was another framed document outlining the rules of the camp.

Dixie had pointed them out. 'I suppose you ought to read these, but I suggest you wait until the morning. In the unlikely event of fire breaking out during the night, I'll make sure you're rescued.'

Eirlys now sat on the bed, and while she rubbed the bump on her forehead she studied Finn's Ten Rules Of Behaviour. She could hear his voice as she read through them.

1. No one to go off alone, but always in pairs. Each pair must make sure someone knows where they are going.
2. Mobile telephones and all hand-held devices to be surrendered on arrival.
3. Respect your neighbours.
4. No practical jokes of any kind permitted.
5. Interference with any of the activities may result in the perpetrator being asked to leave.
6. No pets allowed.
7. Certain areas are out of bounds. The boundary is clearly marked by a fence and markers. No one is permitted to go outside these boundaries.
8. Everyone must assist with the chores, and the rota is placed on the kitchen door daily.

9. Finn's word is final regarding all disputes.

10. Everyone must have fun.

Eirlys had to agree with the sense behind the rules. They were practical and she particularly liked number ten. Gathering up her sponge bag, she went in search of the shower block.

As she finally emerged dressed and ready for the day, she discovered Finn waiting for her outside the visitors' block. 'Good morning,' he said. He raised the brim of his brown felt hat. Today he was wearing a blue and white striped collarless shirt and the ubiquitous cargo pants that seemed to be the uniform of everyone employed on site. His pockets strained with bulky objects that Eirlys presumed were the necessary tools of his trade.

'Good morning,' she returned his greeting, still not sure how to deal with this charismatic but spiky individual.

This morning he was smiling at her as if he meant it, but Eirlys had made up her mind that where Finn Hart was concerned, it paid to be wary. She couldn't forget his embrace with Miranda Hargreaves, a woman who had a husband called Philip.

'I was looking for my son,' she explained.

'He's gone off orienteering.'

'What?'

'That's our word for the beginners' course. It helps you find your way round.'

'Has he had his breakfast?' Eirlys asked.

'I've been reliably informed that he demolished a large bowl of porridge and two slices of toast and marmalade before setting off, so no need to worry on that score.'

'I would have liked to see him before he left.'

'Why?' Finn's disarming reply wrong-footed Eirlys.

'To make sure he slept well,' she floundered, 'and to talk about the day ahead.'

'He's in perfectly safe hands, and there'll be lots of talking about his day ahead with his companions.'

Eirlys blinked uncertainly. How could she explain her fears for her son's welfare without appearing an overprotective mother?

'Have you had your breakfast?' Finn asked her.

'I'm usually happy with coffee,' Eirlys admitted.

'In that case would you care to join me for a cup in the office? We do need to complete your paperwork.'

Unable to think of a reason to refuse Finn's suggestion, and uncertain as to why it should unsettle her, Eirlys nodded.

'We'll collect our own supplies from the kitchen. Hannah and her crew have enough to do without me pestering them for personal service. How do you take your coffee?'

'You're going to make it?' Eirlys fell into step beside him.

'You'd better believe it. Don't worry, my offering won't taste like boiled mud.'

Eirlys perched on one of the chairs in Finn's office while he searched through a pile of papers on his desk. The coffee was fragrant, and Hannah's homemade biscuits melted on the tongue.

'I think the fresh air's sharpened my appetite,' Eirlys explained with an embarrassed smile as she accepted her third biscuit.

Finn cast her a professional glance. 'We need to get some colour into your cheeks. I expect you spend too much time indoors.'

'You mentioned a form?' Eirlys hoped Finn wasn't going to make too many personal remarks.

'I did. Yes. Ah, here it is.' He put out an absent-minded hand, picked up a biscuit and demolished it in two bites. 'I always insist everyone eats breakfast,' he explained with an embarrassed smile, 'but I always forget my own rules, then I wonder why I'm so hungry by lunch-time.'

'Then you'd better drink your coffee before it gets cold,' Eirlys replied.

'Good idea. Want some more?'

The pot was emptied and Finn finished his coffee with a sigh. 'Sorry I can't think of any more excuses to put off the dreaded paperwork — one of my pet hates.' He picked up the sheet of paper on his desk. 'Nothing to worry about, really. I need to know next-of-kin details, if you have any allergies, or suffer from any of the medical conditions listed.'

'I understand.'

'It's a sort of disclaimer too. We do have medical staff on site to deal with any day-to-day complications that may arise, but one thing I've learned is always to expect the unexpected when it comes to young boys. So are you ready?' Eirlys indicated that she was. 'Who is your next of kin?' Finn asked.

'Gareth's grandmother, my husband's mother, Martha Pendragon.'

'You're a single mother?' Finn asked carefully.

'Yes,' Eirlys replied, not wanting to tell Finn about the motorbike accident that had left her a struggling young widow with a two-year-old son to bring up alone.

'We know how you heard about us.' His smile defused the situation as he proceeded down his list of questions, ticking the boxes as he went along. 'Right, well, if you'd like to sign and date the form — unless you have any questions you'd like to ask me?'

'I'd like to know about your business plans for the future,' Eirlys replied. 'Are you seeking corporate investment, or do you intend to carry on as a one-man band?'

Finn's raised eyebrows expressed his astonishment. 'I hadn't expected that one,' he admitted.

'Nonetheless I'd like a reply,' Eirlys said in a calm voice.

'May I know why?'

'I was unable to complete my business studies course, but I'm still interested in all areas of commerce.'

'I see.' Finn capped his pen. 'Gareth tells me you paint for a living?'

'I do. It enables me to work to my own schedule, and I need to be on hand at short notice should emergencies arise. It wouldn't be fair to rely on my mother-in-law all the time. She has her own life to lead.'

'Right, well in answer to your question, as you know it's early days. I have plans to extend the camp, and for that I do need financial support. I don't intend to go into details, but I have one main investor whose identity I also do not intend to reveal.'

'Do you stay open throughout the year?'

'We plan to close during the winter months.'

'How well are you doing?'

'This week we're full, as it's half term. The holidays are always busy, and in term time we arrange school trips and parties, so it's constant coming and going. Now was there anything else?' He held out his hand for Eirlys' signed form. 'By the way, I have a question for you,' he said.

'I've read your rules of behaviour list,' Eirlys replied, 'and I remembered to hang my towel on the right hook in the shower room. I also cleaned my area of the shower and I made my bed. My belongings, such as they are, have been neatly tidied away in the visitors' unit, and I shall now take our coffee tray back to the kitchen, where I shall proceed to wash up the mugs and empty the pot for the next person to use.'

Eirlys couldn't recall a rule about being too lippy with the management, but she suspected Finn could twist them to meet his own ends if it suited him, and if that was the case she might just have blown it.

'I was actually going to ask you if you'd like to call an owl with me this evening.'

'You what?' Eirlys gaped.

'You have to do it after dark, and I thought it was something you might enjoy — that's if you're still here, of course.'

Eirlys found her voice. 'Why shouldn't I be?'

'Things aren't going too well between us, are they? We could use owl-calling as a bonding experience.'

'After dark?'

'That's the only time I've got free. The owls don't do much during the day either. So, Eirlys Pendragon, do you accept my invitation? That's a pretty name, by the way. What does it mean?'

Eirlys swallowed the rising lump in her throat. Her heart was beating in a most uncomfortable manner and she was finding it difficult to think clearly. 'Eirlys? It's Welsh and it means snowdrop.'

Finn nodded approval. 'Ten o'clock this evening? Outside your cabin?'

The ringing of the telephone interrupted their conversation. Finn picked up the receiver, leaving Eirlys to find her way back to the kitchen, wishing she had the courage to refuse his invitation.

3

'Hi there,' Dean Robinson greeted Eirlys as she emerged from Finn's office, her common sense telling her to have nothing to do with night owl-calling, or Finn Hart come to that.

Eirlys frowned at Dean. 'What are you wearing?' His T-shirt and combats were covered in weird khaki and dark green squiggles.

'Camouflage kit,' he explained. 'I'm leading the older boys on an obstacle course. They think it's macho if they dress up for it. I always feel a tad silly, but Finn insists we go with the flow, so — ta da.'

Eirlys, fearing she may have sounded rude earlier, did her best to repair the situation. 'It looks very nice.'

Dean nudged her with his elbow. 'You're just saying that.'

'I am actually,' Eirlys admitted. They

laughed and the tension between them eased.

'How are you settling in?' Dean enquired.

'I slept well, but I haven't seen much of anything yet.'

'Then allow me to escort you round.'

'I wouldn't want to take you away from your obstacle course duties.'

'I've got to check the facilities. I'm on my way to do it now, so why don't you walk the course with me?'

'You're not going to insist I physically test the equipment or anything like that, are you?'

'Scout's honour,' Dean promised solemnly. 'So, do you know who everyone is on site?'

'I've met Miranda Hargreaves,' Eirlys said. Dean pulled a face. 'You don't like her?'

'I didn't say that. Without her I suppose I wouldn't have a job.'

'She's a friend of yours?'

'I didn't say that either.'

'Then how do you know her?'

'Have you met Philip?' he asked.

'Her husband? No, but I've heard mention of him.'

'He's Finn's main backer.'

Eirlys stared at Dean. 'He's invested in the camp?'

'A substantial sum.'

'How can he afford it?'

'He runs his own electronics firm. Despite his corporate image he's a bit of a philanthropist. The competition was actually his suggestion.'

'No kidding?'

'So without Philip you wouldn't be having this lovely holiday in the heart of the forest. Hold this, would you?' He passed over a ball of string. 'Blessed things are always dropping off.'

'What are they for?' Eirlys looked at the cork Dean was clutching in his hand as he reattached it to the string.

'The boys like to know how far they've swung on the rings, so we dangle corks along the side as a measuring device. There, that's better. Now for the water course.'

Eirlys looked down at a ditch situated on the far side of a small fake hedge. The water looked cold and unwelcoming. 'Don't the boys fall in?'

'Not if they take a long enough leap. It isn't deep; and even if they do fall in, they don't seem to mind. It's the most popular challenge on the course.' He tested one of the poles supporting the raised netting rigged over another small pit. 'Want to have a go? There aren't any snakes in the pit.'

Eirlys shivered at the prospect. 'No thanks.'

'Only a joke,' Dean assured her.

'About Philip Hargreaves,' Eirlys probed as they continued their inspection of the course.

'What about him?' Dean made sure the hurdles were the correct height and that the poles would fall out if someone knocked into them.

'Does he mind Miranda working here?'

'She isn't officially on the payroll. She does photos and writes the occasional press release, updates the website, that sort of stuff.'

'She seems very friendly with Finn,' Eirlys said, recalling the intimate scene she'd witnessed on her arrival.

'I know I shouldn't talk about my boss behind his back,' Dean replied, 'but I feel sorry for him.'

'Why's that?' Eirlys asked.

'He doesn't dare upset Philip — but Miranda, well . . . on occasions she can be a nuisance. The same goes for Hugo.'

'Who's Hugo?'

'Their son. He's eight years old and currently the bane of my life.'

'Why?'

'Thinks he owns the place. I haven't caught him breaking any of the rules of behaviour so far, but that's not to say he doesn't stretch the boundaries to their limit. He often stays over and he always upsets people.'

'What sort of things does he do?' The more Eirlys heard about Miranda and her son the more she disliked them.

'I've no proof so I shouldn't really say, but once or twice I've suspected him of tripping people up, especially when they're going over the water course.'

'Why don't you report him?'

'He's crafty, and I'm never too sure of my facts. Besides, who is Finn going to believe — me, or the son of his main benefactor?'

'Point taken,' Eirlys agreed.

They reached the finishing line. 'There. Everything seems to be in order.' He rewound his ball of string.

'Do the boys really enjoy this sort of thing?'

'They love it,' Dean assured her, 'and we don't insist on ice baths afterwards. He grinned. 'That's just for the grown-ups.'

Eirlys shivered. She wasn't exactly sure why. It was a warm day, but that didn't prevent niggles of unease running down her spine.

Dean didn't appear to notice Eirlys' discomfort. 'My cousin gave me lots of pointers for the obstacle course. He plays football — proper league matches — so they have to be in tip-top condition health- and fitness-wise. I scaled everything down for the boys and this is the result.' He glanced at his watch. 'Time for lunch.'

'I've only just had coffee and biscuits with Finn,' Eirlys protested.

'That excuse will not hold water with Hannah, I'm afraid. If you don't finish everything on your plate you'll be washing up all week.'

'You're not serious.'

'No I'm not, but I bet once you've tasted her cottage pie you'll eat every morsel and come back for seconds. Come on. Even if you're not hungry, I am ravenous; and if you really can't manage your tucker I'll help you out.'

A noisy group of boys was sitting on benches outside the cookhouse, laughing and exchanging stories about their morning's activities.

'We eat al fresco as often as possible,' Dean explained. 'The boys like it and it saves on the mess. If they drop anything on the grass it doesn't matter, and there are always accidents.'

'Whose turn is it to wash up today?' Eirlys asked as Dean inspected the rota.

'You're down to do it with Hugo.'

'Miranda's son?' Eirlys felt a pang of apprehension.

'Make sure he pulls his weight,' Dean warned her. 'Given half a chance he'll bunk off.'

'What do I do if he does?'

'You should report him.'

'And who's Finn going to believe?' Eirlys repeated Dean's earlier question.

'Life's a devil at times, isn't it?' Dean commiserated. 'Come on, let's find a seat. Look, there's Gareth waving at you.'

'Mum!' her son shouted from the far end of the table.

'Mind my eardrums, young man,' Hannah admonished him as she dished out generous portions of her cottage pie. 'Your mother's not deaf.'

'Over here,' Gareth called.

Eirlys settled down beside him. 'Have

you had a good morning?'

Was it her imagination, or did a faint shadow cross her son's face?

'We had a great time.'

Another boy joined them and punched Gareth playfully on the shoulder. Eirlys looked at him. There was an expression in his eyes that was disturbingly familiar. 'I'm Hugo Hargreaves.' He grinned in an assured manner. 'Gareth's staying in our cabin and I'm looking after him,' he boasted as he eased himself into the space between Gareth and Eirlys and began to eat the portion of cottage pie that Hannah had placed in front of Gareth.

Hannah raised her eyebrows and doled out another portion. 'Some of us could do with a lesson in manners, young man,' she said.

Hugo looked up at her, his eyes widening in surprise. 'I thought this was my place.'

'What did you see this morning?' Eirlys asked. She didn't want a situation developing that might implicate Gareth. Hugo, she suspected, was adept at talking his way out of trouble. 'We walked the boundaries,' Hugo replied, 'and I showed Gareth the markers indicating how far we're allowed to go.'

'We saw the tumbledown,' Gareth mumbled through a mouthful of cottage pie.

'What's that?' Eirlys asked.

'It's an old cottage,' he began.

'Where no one is supposed to go,' came a deep voice. Eirlys spun round. She hadn't heard Finn approach their table. The expression in his eyes was icy and suggested he had overheard every word of their conversation.

'We didn't go inside,' Hugo was quick to explain, 'but Gareth wanted to see it.'

'It's an unsafe structure and strictly out of bounds,' Finn responded in a voice that sounded as icy as the expression in his eyes.

Eirlys leapt to her son's defence. 'Gareth wouldn't have known that.'

'All the same, can you please make

sure your son reads the rules of behaviour and abides by them?' Finn replied, not giving Eirlys a chance to reply before he moved on to speak to the next table. Outraged, Eirlys could only glare after his retreating figure.

'Does Gareth really live with his grandmother during the week because you haven't got a proper house, only a battered old caravan?' Hugo spoke in a voice loud enough to attract the attention of their fellow diners.

'Hey, that sounds cool,' another boy joined in. 'We went camping last summer and I wanted to sleep in one of the caravans, but they were all booked.'

'Bet you wouldn't want to live in one,' Hugo said, waving his fork in the air.

'I like living with Granny Marcus,' Gareth piped up.

'Granny Marcus?' Hugo taunted. 'What sort of name is that? Is she a man in disguise?'

Eirlys was reluctant to be seen as an interfering mother who leapt to her

41

son's defence every five minutes, but Hugo needed a short sharp lesson in manners.

'I used to have to call my grandmother Two-Nanny,' Dixie laughed before Eirlys could think of a suitable retort. 'She wasn't really my grandmother at all, but she'd married my granddad after his first wife died and she sort of became my second grandmother. I suppose she was my third really, 'cause I had another grandmother as well.'

'What do you call a lot of grannies?' Eirlys was pleased to hear Gareth was laughing again and sent a silent message of thanks with her eyes to Dixie.

'I don't know,' the girl took up Gareth's challenge, 'what do you call a lot of grannies?'

'A granary,' Gareth sniggered.

Everyone laughed, and with Hugo's taunts forgotten they all tucked into Hannah's jam roly poly, which was served with strawberry jam and the biggest jug of custard Eirlys had ever seen in her life.

Dean was at her side as the plates were collected. 'Told you so.'

Despite her biscuit snack, Eirlys had managed to eat a full lunch. 'That was one of the best meals I've had in years,' she admitted.

'It's no good trying to get off washing-up duties by flattering Hannah,' Dixie warned her.

'I wasn't,' Eirlys began, then laughed as she realised the girl was pulling her leg.

'Hey, Hugo,' Dean bellowed, 'no skulking off. You're down to help Eirlys with the dishes.'

'It's not my turn,' he protested.

'Don't argue. Here, take these to the kitchen and make a start on them.'

For a moment Eirlys thought the boy was going to refuse — or worse still, drop the plates — but realising Dean meant business, he sighed and snatched the crockery out of his hands.

'I expect he'll report that to his mother,' Dixie murmured as the boy slouched off.

'Let him,' Dean said. 'Everyone else does their bit. Why should he get away with it?'

'I think you're on obstacle course duty this afternoon, Dean,' Finn interrupted with a pointed look at Dixie.

'And I'm off to help in the laundry,' she reacted with a sweet smile.

Eirlys found herself facing Finn. 'There's no need to remind me I should be doing the dishes.'

'I just wanted to say you've got to make allowances for Hugo,' Finn began.

'If my son had been that rude to a guest I would have sent him to his room with no lunch, but you obviously set a different standard of manners for your charges.'

'You don't understand.'

'I understand only too well, Finn. Hugo's father has the money and money speaks. I suppose that's why you're so . . .' She paused. '*friendly* with Miranda.'

'I'd be grateful if you didn't gossip with the staff,' Finn retaliated. 'They have work to do.'

'And so do I.' She turned on her heel and headed for the kitchen.

4

'Cup your hands and blow,' Finn instructed. 'Like this, through the gap in your thumbs.' He placed his fingers over Eirlys' to demonstrate. With her eyes fixed on his, she blew. Nothing happened. He removed his hands.

'Have another go,' he urged. 'You know what a tawny owl sounds like, don't you?'

'Sort of, but I've never tried to mate one before,' Eirlys couldn't resist responding.

'I'm not suggesting we go that far.' Finn's lips moved with the suggestion of a smile. 'But it's a sight worth seeing when they soar through the night air responding to your call.'

To Eirlys' surprise, Finn had come looking for her after she'd settled Gareth down in his cabin after supper. As well as Hugo there were two other boys sleeping there, one of whom she was pleased to see was the boy who at lunchtime had thought it was cool to live in a caravan. She was also pleased to see it was Archie and not Hugo who shared the bottom half of Gareth's bunk.

'Are we still on for a spot of owl-calling?' Finn had again appeared out of the shadows and caught her on the hop.

'I thought you telephoned the general store in the evening,' she said. A part of her had been hoping he would have forgotten about their date.

'I've done it,' he said. 'There were no specials, so tomorrow's order was purely routine. Ready?'

'About Gareth and the tumble-down . . . ' Eirlys felt compelled to speak up on behalf of her son, but Finn held up a hand to stop her.

'I want everyone to be aware of all possible pitfalls and hazards. The forest can be a dangerous place, and that is why the boys aren't allowed to go out of bounds. Gareth probably didn't realise it was a foolish act to visit the tumbledown, but now I expect it's a mistake he won't repeat.'

'He wouldn't have made it in the first place if it hadn't been for Hugo Hargreaves.'

'He knows the situation too. Now, subject closed. Have you got a jumper and some sensible shoes?'

Realising it would be pointless to continue arguing her son's cause, Eirlys asked, 'Where are we going?'

'Tawny owls like woodland as a natural habitat, so we'll go deeper into the forest. It can get quite cold after the sun goes down. That's why you need to wear something warm.'

'Is anyone else joining us?' Eirlys glanced over his shoulder.

'Lights out by ten; and as most of my charges are more than ready for sleep by then . . . ' He glanced at the dial of his luminescent watch. 'It's five past, so in answer to your question, no.'

★ ★ ★

48

Eirlys disappeared into her cabin to change into stout walking shoes and a jumper and waterproof. She then rejoined Finn, who had been waiting patiently outside. She was glad Finn led the way, as after a few minutes her sense of direction deserted her and she had no idea in which direction they were heading.

'You do know where we're going?' she hissed into the darkness.

'I do, and I've followed my own rules. I told Dean what we were doing, so if we're not back in an hour he'll come looking for us.'

Eirlys was relieved they were only going to be away from base for an hour. Being this close to Finn Hart unsettled her. He swished at the bracken with his walking stick to clear a path for Eirlys as she trailed in his wake until eventually they came to a halt in a small clearing.

Finn pointed into the darkness. 'See the hole in that tree trunk?' Eirlys nodded. 'That's where the owls like to nest.'

'You've seen them?'

'From time to time. Want to have

another go at calling one?'

'What sound am I supposed to make?' Eirlys asked, her initial aversion to the outing forgotten.

'Try a bit of *ooo*,' Finn suggested.

Eirlys narrowed her eyes. 'This isn't a wind-up?' Finn hadn't struck her as an overgrown schoolboy, but with some men you never knew.

'When it comes to the forest I'm deadly serious,' he assured her.

Eirlys obediently re-cupped her hands and blew. A strange sound emerged, and as she took a deep breath preparing for a second blow she caught sight of a pair of wings flapping out of the tree before a graceful silhouette emerged into the darkness.

Finn grabbed Eirlys' arm. 'Success. Look — there she goes.'

'How do you know it's a she?'

'The females are bigger than the males.'

'It's like something out of a television documentary.' Eirlys watched in awe as the bird circled the clearing.

'It's far better than manufactured entertainment, wouldn't you say?' Finn cast her a sideways look.

'And I did it,' Eirlys crowed.

'Knew you'd enjoy the experience,' he said as the owl finished her circuit and returned to her tree.

'Is that it?' Eirlys asked in disappointment.

'We don't want to tire her out. And talking of being tired, I suppose we'd better make our way back.'

'Do you do this often?' Eirlys asked, still trying to get her head round the wonderful sight they'd seen.

'When I get the chance, which isn't often. Most of the parents don't stay over, and those who do don't like getting their feet dirty.'

'Happens to me all the time,' Eirlys replied. 'Dirty feet,' she added.

'So you really do live in a caravan?' Finn enquired as they began to walk back to the camp.

'That's a bit of an exaggeration.' She smiled. 'I do most of my work in the caravan, and occasionally I sleep over if I'm late or if I want to start really early in the morning.'

'Painting?' Finn asked.

'As I explained, I'm a freelance artist. I mostly paint people's pets.'

'Isn't it difficult to get an animal to sit quietly in a caravan?'

'I do a lot of work from photos. If I'm commissioned to do a picture of a house or garden then I work on site if I can.'

'I would've thought that'd be a much easier option.'

'If it's a secret present and the donor doesn't want the recipient to find out what I'm up to, it can cause complications.' Eirlys laughed. 'That has led to some unfortunate situations,' she admitted.

'I can imagine. Where do you live when you're not in your caravan?'

'My mother-in-law's got a bungalow. It can be a crush; that's why I move out every so often, to give her some breathing space. Gareth sleeps over with her.

As Hugo told everyone at lunch, my caravan isn't exactly state-of-the-art.'

'But you like it?'

'I love it. I inherited it from Marcus,' she said in a quiet voice. 'He was training to be a forest ranger.'

They tramped on in silence for a few moments. As if sensing her reluctance to talk about Marcus, Finn changed the subject. 'Are you going to stay all week?'

'Am I not welcome?' Eirlys asked with a quaver in her voice.

'I thought maybe you'd like to go off for a few days and give Gareth a chance to bond with the other boys without parental supervision.'

'I like to spend as much time with him as possible.'

'All the same, don't you think things might be easier for him if you weren't always around?'

'Is this what this outing's been all about?' Eirlys tripped over a tree root as she forgot to look where she was going.

Finn put out a hand. 'Steady.'

Eirlys shook it off her arm. 'I can manage, thank you.'

'I only meant,' Finn began, 'it might be better for Gareth if you let him find his feet. Children are marvellous at adapting to circumstances.'

'For your information, Mr Hart, I do not appreciate being told how to bring up my son. He's a nervous child, and putting him in a cabin with someone like Hugo Hargreaves gives me cause for concern.'

They had now reached the camp boundary and lights from the cookhouse twinkled in the distance.

'He'll be fine.'

'I can find my own way from here.'

'Think about what I've said,' Finn replied in a mild voice. 'Gareth will never shake off his fears if you're always around fighting his cause.'

Leaving him standing by the small gate, Eirlys strode towards the guest cabin, wishing she had the courage to tell him she would be leaving in the morning — but she knew that decision would break her son's heart. He had been so looking forward to being at the camp, and when they heard they'd won the competition he had been incandescent with delight.

'My, you've got a face on you that would sink a thousand ships. Whatever's wrong?' Miranda had appeared from nowhere and stood in front of her. The smell of her perfume clogged the back of Eirlys' throat. 'It's Eirlys Pendragon, isn't it? The waif from the broken-down bus. Don't tell me Finn's been making a nuisance of himself.'

'Of course he hasn't,' Eirlys snapped.

'I suppose he's treated you to a spot of owl-calling?' There was a laugh in her voice as she continued. 'Good old Finn. Never changes his routine. It clearly didn't work on this occasion. Judging by your expression I'd say he went too far.'

'What are you doing here?' Eirlys demanded. 'Isn't it a little late for a social call?'

'I come and go as I please.' Miranda

smiled. 'Finn, what have you been doing to Eirlys? The poor girl looks traumatised.'

'Miranda,' he greeted her, but did not answer her question. 'What's up? The gates are closed to visitors after ten.'

'I've just been explaining to Eirlys that I don't need a reason to drop by, and I'm not your run-of-the-mill visitor.'

'Agreed, but I'm off duty.'

Miranda's eyes narrowed. 'I thought you were always on duty.'

Eirlys backed away just as the ring tone of a mobile telephone interrupted them. 'I'll leave you two to play catch-up.'

There was a malicious glint in Miranda's green eyes as she asked, 'Who's broken the rules of behaviour? No mobiles allowed on site. I left mine in the car. Finn?'

'You know I use my two-way radio to communicate on base.' As if in answer to her query, it crackled with static.

'Then it must be you, Eirlys.' The expression on Miranda's face was that of a cat taunting a mouse. It was pointless denying the accusation. Eirlys always carried her mobile with her so her clients could contact her whenever they wished.

'I'm sorry, Finn,' she apologised. 'I forgot I had it on me.'

'Hand it over,' Miranda said. 'No excuses.'

'It may be an emergency.'

'Not good enough. You should have left the camp number as a contact if you were expecting a call.'

'Why don't you wait in the office, Miranda?' Finn interceded.

'What for?' she asked.

'I want to have a private word with Eirlys.'

'Very well. I'll go chat to Hugo.'

'I'd rather you didn't wake him up.'

'It *is* rather late to be up and about,' Miranda agreed in a voice loaded with meaning. 'All right, I won't stay. I'll call by tomorrow, mid-morning?' Without waiting for an answer, she swung her designer bag over her shoulder, and in a waft of cloying perfume picked her way across the grass back to where she had parked her car.

'I was always taught not to say good night on an argument,' Finn said before Eirlys could speak.

She blinked at him, confused by the expression in his eyes.

'We are still friends?' he asked. Eirlys gave a reluctant nod. 'Shake on it?'

She took his hand in hers. His touch was warm and reassuring.

'Good. I suggest you answer that call,' he said with a slow smile. 'Then if you still wish to remain with us, leave your mobile in the office tomorrow morning. It will be returned to you at the end of your stay.'

Eirlys remained where she was for several moments before reaching into the pocket of her coat to extricate her mobile phone to check on her missed message.

5

Dixie sidled up to Eirlys as they queued for their porridge. Her breath misted the morning air, but no one seemed to mind having breakfast outside as the day promised to be fine and sunny. 'Have you heard?' Dixie asked.

Eirlys clutched her bowl and spoon to her chest, worried what further bad news she was in for.

'I don't think I've broken any more rules, have I?'

'It's Hugo,' Dixie replied.

'What about him?'

'His trainers have gone missing.'

'Is that serious?' Eirlys asked.

'Miranda is kicking up a fuss. Hugo's demanding she buy him a new pair.' She nudged Eirlys in the back. 'Get a move on. The troops are getting restless.'

Realising they had reached the front

of the queue, Eirlys filled up her bowl, added some brown sugar, then picked up her mug. She looked round for Gareth.

'He's already been and gone,' Dixie explained. 'He wanted to be first on the obstacle course. There's no need to look so worried. He's fine. Archie's his new best friend. I think the two of them are joined at the hip. They're doing everything together.'

'Where's Hugo?' Eirlys couldn't see him either.

'Not sure.' Dixie sat down. 'But a word of warning.' Eirlys paused, her spoon halfway to her mouth. 'Don't let him blame Gareth for what occurred — the loss of his trainers?' Dixie clarified.

'Why should Hugo do that? My son wouldn't steal another boy's things.'

'We know that, but Hugo might want to show off in front of the others. The only way he can do that is by picking on someone new.'

'Has anything else gone missing?'

'Not to my knowledge, but Dean and I will keep an eye on things. To be honest, I think Hugo's left them somewhere, and rather than be accused of not looking after his possessions, he's invented the whole story.'

Eirlys pushed away her plate of porridge, her appetite having deserted her. 'I've got to complete a painting commission, and I'm planning on leaving the camp for a couple of days.'

'When?'

'As soon as possible.'

'Have you told Finn?'

'Not yet. We didn't actually part on good terms last night.'

'The owl-calling wasn't a success?' Dixie asked.

'I scored a black mark. I had my mobile with me.'

'And you got a call?' Dixie sympathised. 'Bad luck. I think it's a silly rule, but Finn won't budge. It's the same with animals. He won't allow them on site. He says they could be a hazard and that if they ran around they might cause an accident. I suppose I can understand his reasoning, but I do miss my Polly. She's a Labradoodle, a cross between a Labrador and a poodle. My mum looks after her for me while I'm at work.'

A hungry boy looked longingly at Eirlys' bowl. 'Aren't you going to finish your porridge?'

She shook her head. 'You can have it if you like.' The next moment it was whisked away as if the boy was scared she might change her mind.

'Finn's usually in the office this time of day,' Dixie said, 'if you want to catch him.'

Eirlys found him studying the rota for the coming week. He looked up as she knocked on the door.

'Come to hand in your mobile phone?' he asked with a smile.

'Actually, if it's convenient with you, I'm going to have to leave for a day or two.'

'Not bad news, I hope?' A look of concern crossed his face.

'I was halfway through a commission

when we left. A father wanted me to paint his little girl as a present for his wife, but his wife came back from her business trip early. There was no way he could explain my presence to her without giving the game away, so I suggested he waited until his wife went away again and we could reschedule. I only have today and tomorrow to get the work done. That's what last night's call was about.'

'Do you want a lift somewhere?'

'The client is coming to collect me.'

'Then don't let me detain you further. Gareth will be fine here. I'll keep a special eye out for him. We've quite a few things planned over the coming days.'

'Dixie was telling me that Hugo's trainers have gone missing,' Eirlys began.

'And I've already bought him a new pair.' Miranda breezed into the office clutching an expensive-looking bag sporting a prestigious sportswear logo. 'My, you two do seem to be spending a lot of time together.' She arched an eyebrow. 'What is it this time? Don't tell me Finn's discovered that young Gareth's the culprit?'

Eirlys opened her mouth to protest but Finn forestalled her. 'You'll find Hugo with the raft-building team.'

'I haven't come to see my son.' Miranda deposited the bag on a spare chair. 'We had a meeting, remember? So if you've finished with Eirlys? By the way,' she added, looking at Eirlys, 'there's a man looking for you in reception. I followed his car down the drive. I didn't realise you moved in such exalted circles. He was driving a top-of-the-range Jag, no less.'

Finn nodded at Eirlys. 'You'd better go. I'll tell Gareth for you.'

She could hear Miranda's low laugh as she closed the office door behind her.

Dixie rushed over, hardly able to catch her breath as Eirlys, still fuming over the implication that Gareth had taken Hugo's trainers, was heading towards reception. 'Are you going my way?' Dixie asked. 'Only, I need a lift.'

'What's happened?' Eirlys enquired with a pang of concern, temporarily forgetting her annoyance. Dixie's hair was a mess and she was looking wildly from side to side, not really listening to Eirlys.

'My mother's been on the telephone. Polly — you remember my dog?'

'The Labradoodle?'

'She's been involved in an accident. I've been given leave to go and see her, only the camp transport is out on a call. You mentioned something about a commission, and that you were going to leave this morning?'

'According to Miranda my client's in reception, so if he's agreeable I'm sure we can offer you a lift.'

Dixie swung her backpack over her shoulder. 'Dean's promised to keep an eye on Gareth in our absence, so he'll be fine. Come on. Let's go.'

★ ★ ★

Brian Jackson readily agreed to take Dixie to the nearest bus station, after which he drove Eirlys to his large country house, a period property set in secluded grounds an hour's drive from Finn's Forest.

'Was that Miranda Hargreaves I saw mincing through reception?' he asked with a mild smile as they pulled up outside the house. 'She's a friend of my wife's,' he explained, 'and I've had occasional business dealings with her husband.'

'Hugo is staying at the camp,' Eirlys explained.

'Don't, for heaven's sake, let on to Jenny that you've been staying there too,' he pleaded.

'Whyever not?' Jenny was Brian's daughter and the subject of Eirlys' commission.

'She's enraged that Finn's Forest doesn't accept girls and is forever on at me to do something about it. You haven't got daughters, have you?' Eirlys shook her head in reply to his question.

'It's very difficult to refuse them anything, but this time she's got me stumped.' He opened the passenger door of his car. 'Anyway, here we are. Best get down to it before my wife gets back.'

* * *

The commission went well and Eirlys was pleased to put the finishing touches to the portrait ahead of schedule. Despite Brian's words of warning, his daughter had been very placid, and as long as she was allowed to play with her toy pony, was content to sit on a stool to have her portrait painted.

'You've done a wonderful job,' Brian enthused the next day. 'I hope you slept well in the housekeeper's quarters?'

'She made me very welcome, thank you,' Eirlys replied, wishing Finn Hart would take a leaf out of Brian Jackson's book. When it came to manners, the two men could not be more different.

'Excellent. The painting will make a

lovely present for my wife. If you want a recommendation, please don't hesitate to ask me. I've added a little extra to the amount we agreed.'

'That isn't necessary,' Eirlys responded as she tidied up her palette and brushes.

'I thought perhaps you could buy something for Gareth. I know how expensive children of that age can be.' The man smiled and nodded in the direction of his daughter. 'There's always something, isn't there? And no sooner have you bought it before it's too small or they've moved on to something else. 'It's so yesterday' is one of Jenny's favourite sayings.'

Eirlys accepted the envelope he passed over. 'That's very kind of you. Gareth is in need of new trainers. He's only got a very old pair, and some of the boys up at the camp have been teasing him because they're not state-of-the-art.'

'How are you getting on?' Brian Jackson asked. 'I'd heard Finn Hart's a pioneer in that direction.'

Eirlys hesitated. 'Some of the boys come from a different background to Gareth. Most of them are kind and thoughtful.'

'But things like having the right trainers counts?' Brian queried.

Eirlys replaced the last of her brushes in the container. 'I'm afraid so.'

'Would you like me to drive you into town? We could go on a shopping spree.'

'I wouldn't want to put you to any trouble,' Eirlys insisted.

'It would be no trouble, and I could offer some advice on what young boys like. I mean, I wouldn't presume to infer that a mother doesn't know best, but sometimes a masculine input can put a different slant on things.'

'You mean in case I fancy some with pink laces?' Eirlys laughed. She liked Brian Jackson. He and his wife struck her as a lovely couple, and their daughter was an equally likeable child. It made a pleasant change to talk to someone who wasn't on their own agenda and, although he was a busy man, Brian was also generous with his time.

'I have to visit the bank, so you wouldn't be taking me out of my way, and my housekeeper is quite happy to look after Jenny in my absence. I'll run you back to the camp afterwards, unless you have other plans?'

Once in town, Eirlys realised her art supplies were running low, and the excellent local shop was fully stocked.

'Tell you what,' Brian Jackson suggested, 'why don't you get all that you want, then we can make a detour via your caravan where you can offload your bits and pieces.'

'You've done far too much for me already,' Eirlys protested. 'We're running behind schedule as it is.'

'Then why don't we go the whole hog and have some lunch? You hardly ate a thing for breakfast.'

'I wanted to get on with the portrait.'

'A sentiment I thoroughly endorse, but I'm not having you fainting on me for lack of sustenance.' As if endorsing his words, the clock on the town hall struck half past two.

Eirlys stared up in surprise at the Victorian tower. 'Is that the time?'

'Exactly. Now I know an excellent pizzeria that does the best toppings anywhere, so let's get this stuff loaded in the car, have something to eat, then sort ourselves out for the rest of the afternoon.'

'This is most generous of you,' Eirlys replied as Brian refused to accept a contribution towards the cost of lunch as the waitress brought their bill. 'And not what we agreed.'

'I had an ulterior motive,' he admitted. 'I was starving. My wife's been on a diet — something to do with a new dress she wants to fit into for a family wedding. We've been eating nothing but salads for months. I mean, I like lettuce and tomato, but occasionally I long for something more substantial. I'm glad to see you have a healthy appetite for one so small. Now would you like some more coffee, or another slice of gâteau to go with it?'

'I couldn't.' She leaned back against her chair with a satisfied sigh.

'In that case, if you're ready, shall we leave?'

⋆   ⋆   ⋆

'What a lovely spot.' Brian drove his car into the farmer's field and came to a halt by Eirlys' green-painted caravan. The small windows gleamed from their constant polishing, and sprigged curtains decorated the door.

'I love it here,' Eirlys admitted. 'The farmer lets me stay rent-free if I promise to check all the gates are shut. There's a public right of way through the field and not everyone follows the country code of practice.'

'How long have you lived here?' Brian asked as he retrieved the shopping from the boot.

'On and off ever since I got married.' She unlocked the door. 'I would ask you in, but I'm afraid there isn't much room. Most days I work outside under an awning.'

'Shall I pass the stuff through?' Brian suggested, struggling with a large canvas.

'Thank you.'

They worked diligently for several moments.

'Is that your mobile or mine?' Brian asked as a ring tone burst into life.

'It sounds like mine,' Eirlys answered from deep inside the caravan. 'Can you answer it?' she asked. 'I left my bag on the seat of your car.'

A few moments passed before Brian returned to the caravan, a concerned look on his face. 'That was Finn Hart,' he said.

Eirlys dropped the canvas she was holding.

'There's been an accident at the camp.'

6

'Where's Gareth?' Eirlys pounced on Hannah the cook, after Brian Jackson had broken every motoring record to return her to the camp. Her voice had reached fever pitch, but the woman facing her didn't seem that concerned about the boy.

'In the sick bay,' Hannah answered calmly. Her further attempts to speak were futile as Eirlys raced out of the kitchen towards the medical unit.

Finn was standing by a desk talking to a duty nurse as she crashed through the doors. 'Gareth?' she gasped, and fell into Finn's arms.

'He's fine,' he assured her with a hug.

She sobbed, scarcely able to breathe. 'You said he fell and broke his arm.'

'Mrs Pendragon,' the nurse interrupted in a firm voice, 'Mr Hart implied nothing of the sort and that is not the message he conveyed. Your son has suffered no more than a minor sprain to his wrist.'

'I thought to be on the safe side I'd call the doctor in to check him over,' Finn added his explanation to that of the nurse. 'I think the message got garbled in transmission.'

'I want to see my son.'

'He's asleep,' the nurse replied, the tone of her voice indicating she had no intention of disturbing her charge.

'Then wake him up,' Eirlys insisted.

'You don't mean that,' Finn murmured in her ear. 'Why don't we leave Jackie to get on with her job? She'll be on duty all night.'

'And I promise I'll keep a careful eye on your son.' Her expression thawed somewhat now Eirlys had stopped firing accusations at her. 'And if Gareth wakes up I'll call you.'

Eirlys turned on Finn. 'How? You've banned mobiles on site. I've never heard of such a stupid rule in my life.'

His chest was a hard wall against her hands. 'There's an intercom connection to my office. Now come along; I've asked Hannah to make us some tea. We'll go to the quiet room, where we won't be disturbed. Thanks, Jackie,' he called over his shoulder as he guided Eirlys out of the medical unit.

The quiet room was situated away from the main complex in a peaceful part of the compound. Hannah had already placed a tray of tea on a side table and Finn poured out two cups, stirring in a spoonful of sugar. 'Good for shock,' he explained.

Eirlys grimaced. 'I don't sweeten my tea.'

'Today is an exception.'

'What happened?' she demanded.

The cup of tea rattled in its saucer. Finn gently removed it from her grasp and placed it on the table. 'Gareth tripped over and fell awkwardly. Dean saw it happen and was immediately onto it. He called a paramedic and the rest you know.'

'Is it broken, his wrist?'

'No. Gareth is sporting a huge bandage which he'll no doubt boast about tomorrow to the other boys, when I'm sure he'll be as right as rain.'

'Hugo didn't trip him up, did he?'

Finn narrowed his eyes. 'That's a serious allegation and totally without foundation.'

'Is it? I know how you feel about Miranda, and that you think her son can do no wrong. Is that why you turn a blind eye to his failings?'

'I'll pretend I didn't hear that remark,' Finn replied. 'Perhaps you'd better drink your tea before it gets cold.'

Aware she might have overstepped the mark, Eirlys sipped at her tea. 'Sorry,' she murmured.

'Apology accepted,' Finn replied.

'I didn't mean to be rude to Jackie either.'

'She'll understand, and Gareth couldn't be in better hands. Why don't we talk about something else?'

'Such as?'

'I don't know. Who was the man who answered your mobile for a start?'

'Brian Jackson? He's the commission I was telling you about. We'd been out to lunch and to do some shopping.'

'Shouldn't you have been painting his daughter — or was it his dog?'

'His daughter. She was such a good sitter I finished early. Brian offered me a lift into town. He had some business to attend to and I needed to do some shopping, and he was quite willing to stow my bits and pieces in his car. Then I realised I wouldn't be able to bring everything back to the camp due to lack of space, so Brian — Mr Jackson — suggested we stop by the caravan to leave the shopping and check up on things. That's why I didn't take the call. My handbag was in his car. Brian picked up the phone.'

'I see.' It was impossible to tell what Finn from thinking from the tone of his voice.

Eirlys gasped and put a hand to her cheek. 'I left the caravan unlocked. I'll have to call Jack. He's got a key.'

'All in good time,' Finn said. 'And who's Jack?' he asked with another puzzled frown.

'The farmer. It's his field.'

'There do seem to be rather a lot of men in your life,' Finn remarked.

'There's no man in my life in the way you mean,' Eirlys snapped.

'And what way is that?'

Eirlys ignored the question. 'Besides, what business is it of yours how many men there are in my life?'

'None at all,' Finn assured her, then added with a roguish smile, 'But at least I've taken your mind off Gareth. You're going to have to apologise to Jackie for almost assaulting her. She's actually a very kind lady and a good nurse.'

'I shouldn't have left Gareth here on his own.'

'That's nonsense. All boys like a bit of rough and tumble. It's part of the growing up process.'

'I can't help worrying about him.'

'Why?'

'Lots of reasons.'

'Tell me one.'

'He's small, so he gets picked on at school.'

'He won't get picked on here,' Finn said firmly.

'He doesn't like heights. Neither do I.'

'He won't ever conquer that fear if you foster it, and you won't either. The only way to deal with a fear is to face up to it.'

Eirlys' retort died on her lips. The expression on Finn's face wasn't confrontation but concern. 'Let's start with you. Why are you afraid of heights?' he asked.

'I fell out of a tree when I was eight,' she began to explain. 'The school bully dared me to climb it.'

'That explains a lot.' Finn paused.

'It does?'

'Children are very intuitive. Gareth's picked up on your emotion and that probably explains his fear of heights.'

'Do you think so?'

'I have an idea. If you're up for it we can conquer this phobia together.'

Eirlys swallowed the rising lump of nerves in her throat. 'What exactly have you got in mind?'

'Why don't you come out on the zip wire and show Gareth there's nothing to be afraid of?'

'What's the zip wire?'

'We fix a wire up between two trees and attach a harness to it. You get in the harness and away you go. The boys love it. It's like flying.'

Eirlys shuddered. 'You mean whizz from one tree to another all on my own?'

'You've got the picture.'

'I couldn't.'

'You'd be a great example to follow.'

'I'd freeze.'

'Even better. If any of the boys were feeling nervous and saw how you overcame the collywobbles they'd be very impressed and it would encourage them to do the same thing. With you as their role model they'd know it was safe. Think of it as the opportunity of a lifetime.'

It was difficult not to be carried away by Finn's enthusiasm, and Eirlys' fear of heights had always been a neurosis she had wanted to overcome. 'Will you be there?'

'Of course. Dean as well, if you like,

and any of the other rangers we can rope in. There's no chance you'll come to any harm.'

'I suppose I could give it a try,' Eirlys agreed slowly.

'That's my girl. Tomorrow afternoon?'

'So soon?' Eirlys echoed.

'Less time for you to chicken out.'

'What about Gareth? He won't be able to take part.'

'Agreed, but I'm sure he'll be cheering you along with the rest of them. You'll see. It'll raise his street cred no end.'

★ ★ ★

'I feel sick,' Eirlys confided to Dean as he fixed the harness round her waist. They were both standing on the tree platform supporting the structure. Eirlys was doing her best not to look down. They were only a few feet off the ground, but as far as Eirlys was concerned it could have been the Grand Canyon beneath them. She swayed and clung onto Dean's arm.

'It's not too late to back out. We'd all understand,' he sympathised.

'And have everyone thinking I was wetter than a damp weekend?' Eirlys drew herself up to her full height, the light of fire in her eyes. 'No way.'

'That's the spirit,' Dean enthused. 'OK, everything's ready, checked and super-checked. Any last requests?' He held up his hands in a gesture of reconciliation. 'Only joking. Go get 'em.'

Before Eirlys had time to realise what was happening, Dean activated the controls. There was a rush of air and she was sailing down the wire. Her shriek of fear turned to one of delight as she reached her destination to a round of rousing cheers. Several of the boys threw their beanies in the air and whooped with glee.

Eirlys' legs were still trembling, not from fear but excitement and a sense of achievement. Finn undid the harness and helped her out of it.

Gareth, his arm still bandaged, ran over with an excited Archie in tow. 'You did it, Mum.'

'Weren't you scared?' Archie asked, his eyes wide with admiration as Eirlys knelt down to give Gareth a hug, careful not to hurt his wrist.

'There's nothing to it.' Over her son's shoulder her eyes met Finn's. 'In fact, I might have another go.'

'I think you're in for a long wait,' Finn laughed. 'There's a queue building up. Dean looks as though he's got his hands full with that lot.'

A friendly squabble had broken out as to whose turn it was next and Dean had to raise his voice in order to be heard. 'All in good time, guys,' he bellowed. 'Now, smallest first.'

'When can I have a go, Finn?' Gareth demanded. 'My wrist doesn't hurt. Really. Can I take my bandage off?'

'Not without medical supervision,' he insisted.

'Finn,' he protested.

'Don't argue, darling,' Eirlys admonished him. 'You want to get better, don't you?'

'The bandage is hot and it itches.'

'We'll see what Nurse Jackie can do tonight. Meanwhile, why don't you and Archie see if you can find some nice flat stones for the skimming competition? No going too near the water, mind,' Finn insisted.

'Come on, Gareth.' Archie raced off. 'Bet I can find more than you.'

'No you won't.' Gareth set off in hot pursuit.

'I see Gareth's got some state-of-the-art trainers.'

'I bought them out of the bonus Brian gave me. They're not Hugo's missing trainers, if that's what you're thinking,' Eirlys retaliated.

'Whatever you may think of my relationship with Miranda Hargreaves, it doesn't blind me to Hugo's character,' Finn replied.

'What does that mean?' Eirlys shivered, her joy at completing the zip wire contest already evaporating.

'I am well aware Hugo is overindulged and an attention-seeker, but he is still a child and hopefully he'll grow out of his faults.'

'You took his side against Gareth over that business with the tumble-down.'

'I wanted Gareth to realise the rules are there for a reason. He's an intelligent child, and should anyone suggest such an escapade again I'm convinced he won't be swayed into doing anything silly.'

'It was his first day. Hugo's older than him and Gareth placed his trust in him. He deserved your support.'

'I'm not much of a child psychologist, but if he encounters any further challenges I believe Gareth will come out on top. That's why I'm keen to encourage independence in all the boys, even Hugo.'

The sound of laughter floated through the trees. 'It sounds like they're having fun,' Eirlys said.

'The simplest pleasures are often the best. Have you ever splashed through a puddle or buried someone in the sand?'

'I hope you're not going to suggest

we have a go at that as well,' Eirlys replied. 'I gave up doing that sort of thing when I was twelve. By the way, Miranda says you take all the mothers owl-calling.'

A shadow crossed Finn's face. 'Let's leave Miranda out of this.'

'Is it true?'

'Is what true?'

'Do you go owl-calling with other females?'

'You're not the first,' Finn admitted.

'And I expect I won't be the last.' Eirlys picked up her coat, annoyed with herself for having softened in her attitude towards Finn. 'I'd better get back and see if Hannah needs any help in the kitchen.'

'Look out, Finn,' Dean called out as the zip wire began to turn, 'customer on the way down.'

Taking advantage of the distraction, Eirlys slipped away. She caught sight of a shadowy figure flitting through the trees. Something about the way it was moving convinced her the perpetrator was up to no good. Careful not to step on any twigs to alert the shadow to her presence, she followed it down to the lake.

'Hey,' she heard a howl of protest, 'they're mine.'

'Give them back.' Gareth's raised voice was enough to galvanise Eirlys into action.

Not caring now how much noise she made, she crashed through the undergrowth just in time to see Hugo hurling Archie and Gareth's pebbles back into the lake.

7

'My son has a black eye,' Miranda shrieked at Eirlys, 'and it's all your fault.'

Eirlys was still basking in the pleasure of having seen Archie tackle Hugo and bring him down after he'd disrupted their game of skimming stones. Her heart had been in her mouth as Gareth raised his bandaged arm in protest, but Archie had got to Hugo first and hit his knees with a branch, then rolled on top of him.

The noise had brought Dean and Finn dashing through the trees. They found Eirlys doing a victory dance with her son and Hugo howling in anguish.

'What on earth's going on?' Finn demanded.

'Hugo started it.' Gareth pointed at the older boy. Archie had rolled away from his adversary and he and Gareth now high-fived in delight.

'They punched me.' Hugo was holding his nose in a theatrical gesture of injury.

'No more than you deserved,' Eirlys butted in. 'I saw it all.'

'What happened?' Finn repeated his question.

'I think we need to get everyone back to the medical unit for a checkup,' Nurse Jackie insisted after someone had the foresight to fetch her and alert her to the trouble brewing before things got out of hand. 'Explanations can wait. Now come along, young man, and stop that whining.'

Hugo had shuffled to his feet and trailed after Jackie, doing his best to walk with a convincing limp.

'Other leg,' Archie called after him. 'I hit your left knee, not your right one.'

'That's enough.' Eirlys was pleased to see there was a twinkle in Nurse Jackie's eyes as she reprimanded the boy.

Eirlys was now seated opposite Finn

in his office, Miranda at his side, a look of outrage on her face. 'Your son is a hooligan.' Miranda's green eyes narrowed in anger.

'No more than yours.'

'I said as an experiment the competition thing would never work, Finn.'

'Then you should have spoken to your husband,' Eirlys butted in. 'It was his idea. Are you saying Philip doesn't know what he's talking about?'

'How can you sit there, Finn, and let this woman and her son insult my family?'

'It is three against one,' Finn replied. 'All the witnesses tell the same story.'

'What utter nonsense.'

'You weren't there, Miranda. Eirlys was; and it was Archie, not Gareth, who tackled Hugo. Are you saying Archie isn't the right sort of person to be in the camp either?' A look of devilment came into Finn's eyes. 'I believe he goes to Hugo's school. I expect you know his mother.'

Miranda was now very pink in the

face. 'I suppose you're on Eirlys' side, just because she bats her baby-blue eyes at you and treats you like a hero.'

'I do not.' Eirlys didn't think she had ever been so insulted in her life. The idea of batting her eyes at any man made her feel sick.

'And I'm impartial,' Finn insisted, 'but if Hugo wants to stir things up, I don't think the other boys can be blamed for retaliating — and that's exactly what happened on this occasion. I'd call it character-building, wouldn't you?'

'No, I would not.'

'By the way, Nurse Jackie informs me Hugo's eye wasn't touched in the skirmish. Archie's fist came into contact with his nose; otherwise, he was unscathed.'

'You haven't heard the last of this.' Miranda snatched up her bag and stormed out.

'Have I made things difficult for you?' Eirlys asked in a small voice.

'Only if Philip Hargreaves decides to take things further. He's the power-house in that family.'

'Then I have, haven't I?'

Finn cast Eirlys a speculative look. 'I suppose you've heard I wouldn't be able to run this place without his help?' Eirlys nodded. 'Philip is a major investor, although to his credit he tends to take a back seat and let me get on with it.'

'Would it make things easier for you if Gareth and I left?'

'Not at all. Despite Miranda's threats, Philip wants to encourage boys from all backgrounds to enjoy country pursuits.'

'Including those boys who live with their grandmother during the week because their mother earns her living by painting in a caravan?'

'Especially those boys who have fewer advantages in life. If you leave, Philip will regard his experiment as a failure. He may lose enthusiasm, and I wouldn't want that to happen.'

'I'm not sure I like being referred to as an experiment,' Eirlys objected.

'Sorry, I didn't mean to cause offence.' Finn raised his shoulders in a gesture of apology. 'But you do see my point?'

'Sort of,' Eirlys conceded.

'If Gareth fits in well, which it seems he has, then Philip is considering setting aside funds for a trust, or something along those lines. It's early days and the details would have to be ironed out.'

'Can Miranda stop her husband doing that?'

'She'll probably give it a try. It doesn't help that Hugo requires constant supervision. Miranda isn't around all of the time.'

'Except to accuse my son of being a hooligan.'

'Philip travels a lot as well, leaving Hugo to his own devices. He's an only child, so he's always looking for diversions.'

'Did his trainers really go missing?'

Finn paused. 'I think I should tell you that other things have gone missing.'

'Such as?'

'Nothing of any value. One of the boys asked me to get a birthday card for his mother from the village shop. When he came to write it we couldn't find it anywhere. Then a torch and some batteries disappeared from the store cupboard. Again they could have been misplaced, but so far no one's found them either.'

'I don't have to tell you Gareth wouldn't steal, do I?'

'It never entered my head.'

'He's not a materialistic boy. His grandmother helps out with things like school clothes, but I've no money to spare for expensive extras. That's why he was so thrilled when I was able to buy him those trainers out of the bonus Brian Jackson gave me.'

In the distance a gong sounded.

'Half past six. Time for supper.' Finn stood up. 'Hope you're in good voice.'

'Why?'

'There's going to be a sing-song round the camp fire tonight. We've booked a folk singing duo to get things going. They're very good and always looking for volunteer soloists.'

'Then you are going to be unlucky. I was told to mime the words to the school anthem because I was always flat and I put everyone else off,' Eirlys admitted. 'So if you're looking for a star turn you're out of luck.'

'Well you can join in the chorus. They're always very rowdy and everyone's hopelessly out of tune.' Finn's smile curved the corners of his generous mouth, although his brown eyes held a hint of fatigue. 'Aren't you glad you're staying on?'

'I wasn't aware I had agreed to stay on,' Eirlys replied, determined to keep the exchange as light as possible.

The atmosphere between them was now electrically charged.

'But you will, won't you?' Finn coaxed. 'The boys were so impressed by your performance on the zip wire.'

'Really?' His words caused a warm glow in the pit of Eirlys' stomach. So much had happened since the big event of her afternoon that she had almost forgotten her earlier trial.

'I hope your nerves have recovered.'

'You'd better believe it.' She smiled. 'In fact, I may even have a go at the obstacle course.'

'Don't get carried away by your own success,' Finn laughed. 'You could be seriously embarrassed if you fell in the water ditch, and let me tell you there's a camp tradition that when you fall in you are on your own.'

'You mean no one will fish me out?'

'Nope. It's one of our legendary pursuits, and very popular with the boys, apart from the poor sap who's fallen in of course. There's no chance of anyone drowning, by the way. The water's nowhere near deep enough; but it can get quite muddy, and you know how boys adore dirt.'

'Dean didn't tell me any of this.'

They headed towards the crackling flames of the campfire. 'You like Dean, don't you?'

'He and Dixie are good with Gareth.'

'May I ask you a personal question?'

The light under the trees was fading from the day and Eirlys found it impossible to read the expression on Finn's face. He made a small movement towards her.

'As long as I don't have to answer it.' She backed off.

'It's about Gareth's father.'

They stopped walking and Eirlys took a deep breath. Although Gareth had only been a baby at the time, she still found it difficult to talk about the accident.

'It's just that Gareth seems so much at home in the forest, yet you said in your competition entry he didn't know much about woodland pursuits. You're an artist, which is not always classed as an outdoor pursuit, so I wondered if his father was involved with trees in any way.'

'Gareth feels at home here because Marcus, his father, was training to be a forest ranger.' Eirlys held up a hand to stem Finn's interruption. 'One night he accepted a pillion ride on a fellow student's motorbike. The road was wet and the rider lost control and spun off the road. No one knows what really happened. Gareth was only a baby at the time.'

As she finished speaking, Eirlys was unaware of the birds squabbling in the trees above them, and the excited chatter of the boys as they settled down to supper. It was as if she and Finn were alone in a forest of their own.

'You must have been very young, too.'

'I was married at seventeen. Marcus and I grew up in the same Cornish village. Both our fathers were fishermen, but after Marcus lost an uncle to the sea he decided to do something completely different. We both loved this part of the world, so we moved as far away from the sea as we could. Marcus's widowed mother came with us and Marcus is the reason I abandoned my business studies. Corny as it sounds, we couldn't live without each other.'

'I feel as though I've intruded into

your personal life, but thank you for telling me,' Finn said.

'Have you been married?' Eirlys felt emboldened to ask.

'Until now I've not met the right woman, but life might be a lot easier if I had a wife. Would you ever think of marrying again?'

Eirlys stared at him in dismay, hoping against hope he wasn't thinking of her as a suitable wife.

Dixie jogged over. 'There you are, Finn. I've been looking for you everywhere. I'm reporting back for duty.' She stopped speaking as she caught the expression on Eirlys' face. 'Sorry, did I interrupt something?'

'Not at all,' Eirlys replied, doing her best to recover her equilibrium. 'How's your dog?' She hoped her voice wasn't too shaky.

'Fully up and running again, thank you. Hey, what's been going on here in my absence? I understand poor old Gareth's been in the wars, and the other boys are full of some story about

100

a drama by the lake involving poor old Hugo getting his comeuppance. Archie's being treated as a hero and Hugo's having a monster sulk, so I guess he came out the loser.'

Another figure appeared behind Finn. 'Can I have a word?' Dean murmured in his ear.

Finn spun round. 'About what?' he asked in an urgent voice, seeing the expression on Dean's face.

'One of the supports on the rope bridge doesn't look right, but I know I checked it earlier.'

'Are you saying it's been interfered with?'

'I'd like you to take a look.'

'Don't hold up supper on my account,' Finn told the two women, then strode away with Dean.

'That doesn't sound good,' Dixie admitted.

'Surely no one would sabotage the bridge?' Eirlys replied.

'I agree, and it's not really possible to do any significant damage, but Finn's a stickler for rules. He's bound to report Gareth's accident to the health and safety authorities, and if there is a problem with the bridge they'll have to know about that too.'

'Gareth only sprained his wrist,' Eirlys insisted, 'and nothing has happened on the bridge.'

'All the same, they'll probably want to carry out an inspection. Let's hope we can keep anything else that may happen under wraps.'

'I won't tell anyone,' Eirlys promised.

'We won't be able to hide Hugo's bruised nose and he's bound to big it up if he thinks it'll make him the centre of attention. Nurse Jackie keeps meticulous records too, all available for inspection by the authorities.'

A fragrant smell of vegetable stew wafted towards them.

'Perhaps we're worrying unduly.' Dixie put a reassuring hand under Eirlys' arm. 'The boys seem happy enough, and there's certainly nothing wrong with their appetites.'

'Miranda wasn't too happy about Hugo's accident.'

'A punch on the nose was the best thing that could have happened to her son. He's had it coming to him for ages. By the way, have his trainers come to light?'

'That's something else Finn's got to worry about. There's been a spate of petty pilfering.'

'Hi, Dixie,' Archie said, waving. 'Come and sit next to me. Eirlys, you've got to sit next to Nurse Jackie. She wants to hear all about the zip wire, and I want to tell Dixie exactly what happened by the lake.'

'Do you foresee a glittering future for that young man?' Dixie laughed. 'He's brilliant at getting people to do things, and if push comes to shove he's handy with his fists too.'

'Quite a combination any business-man would be proud of,' Eirlys agreed.

As she sat down she felt a motherly pang of sympathy for Hugo, who was seated opposite her. No one was talking to him and his nose did look rather pink.

'Aren't you staying for the sing-song?' Nurse Jackie asked as he pushed away his plate of uneaten stew.

'Sing-songs are for babies,' he said, 'and I'm tired.' He hesitated, as if hoping someone would ask him to change his mind; but as no one registered a protest, he had no choice but to shuffle back to his cabin on his own.

8

The following day passed without incident, and Eirlys was beginning to hope things were settling down. The pallor in Gareth's cheeks had been replaced by a healthy outdoor glow. His legs, too, looked sturdier, but to his absolute disgust Nurse Jackie insisted he continue to wear a support around his wrist.

'Why?' he complained to his mother. 'It doesn't hurt anymore, and everyone's seen it now.'

'Jackie knows best,' Eirlys insisted after their visit to the medical unit.

'Can I take it off when the inspectors arrive?' he asked hopefully.

Eirlys tripped over the protruding root of a tree as they made their way to the log den Dean was helping the boys construct down by the lake.

'Inspectors?' she repeated as casually

as possible, rubbing at her ankle to cover her confusion.

Gareth put a hand over his mouth in horror. 'I wasn't supposed to say anything.'

'How did you find out about it?' Eirlys asked in a careful voice, not wanting Gareth to betray a trust but at the same time anxious to know about this official visit.

'Archie overheard Finn talking to Dean. He didn't mean to, but the window was open. He swore me to secrecy.'

'Do you know when the inspectors are due?'

'You won't tell anyone, will you?' Gareth pleaded. 'I wouldn't want to get Archie into trouble.'

'I promise.'

'This afternoon. Can I go now?'

Gareth scampered off down the path that led to the lake. Eirlys collected the damp towels from the hooks outside the shower unit and carried them across to the laundry.

One of the assistants took them from her. 'You're on duty today, are you? Shouldn't take long; there aren't many. I reckon some of the little tykes are trying to get away without having a shower. You know how small boys feel about soap and water.'

They were through in less than an hour, and Eirlys unexpectedly found herself with time on her hands. Taking a break, she made a coffee in the kitchen, then strolled out into the sunshine and sat by the remains of the previous night's campfire to drink it. A circle of smoke curled upwards in a fragrant spiral of dying ash. Lost in her thoughts, Eirlys didn't notice a figure emerge from the visitors' car park until a thump on the bench next to her jolted her out of her reverie.

'I hope you're satisfied.'

To her dismay, she realised the new arrival was Miranda, and she was also laden down with cameras and a bulging backpack.

'I'm sorry?'

'Don't tell me this wasn't your doing or that you don't know anything about it.'

'I don't,' a mystified Eirlys insisted, wondering what transgression Miranda was going to accuse her of now.

'Finn's been on the telephone to Philip. He was lucky to catch him at home. He was about to leave for Germany on a business trip. Anyway, I listened in on the extension. It was pretty explosive stuff. Philip was not best pleased.'

'About what?'

'Things were going swimmingly until you arrived. Now we've got accidents, petty theft, strange goings-on and inspectors swarming all over the place — not to mention the trouble you're causing poor Finn, who is too much of a gentleman to say he finds your attentions embarrassing.'

'My attentions?'

'Fawning all over him. What is it with you? Can't you leave the man alone?'

Eirlys clenched her hands, determined not to rise to Miranda's bait.

'Inspectors?' she enquired innocently. 'Is that why you're here?'

'I've been told to repair the damage you've caused.'

'The damage I've caused?'

'It was Philip's idea.'

'What was?'

'He wants some promotional photos for the website. I tried to explain it wasn't convenient and that today is my day for the golf club, but he wasn't having any of it. He said it was time I earned my retainer.' Miranda's husband was clearly a man who stood no nonsense from his wife, Eirlys thought.

'Hadn't you better be getting on with it then?' she suggested.

'Philip wants a feature on Gareth. To do that I need a disclaimer from you.'

Eirlys finished her coffee, then stood up.

'Where are you going?' Miranda asked in an astonished voice.

'Back to the laundry.'

'But I need your help. The disclaimer?'

Eirlys played for time. 'When are the inspectors due?'

'After lunch.'

'Then I'll join you later down by the lake. Meanwhile, I'm busy.' She left a gaping Miranda sitting on her bench looking as if Eirlys had punched her in the stomach.

★ ★ ★

To Eirlys' surprise, the inspectors were quite young, and not the suited and booted individuals she was expecting. The three of them wore casual cargo pants and denim jackets and struck up a rapport with the boys and the staff.

'Ignore us,' the senior inspector insisted to Finn. 'We'll make our own way round the camp. It's what we do to get a feel of the place.'

Apart from an unfortunate incident when a football appeared out of nowhere and hit one of the inspectors on the arm, everything went well. Miranda fluttered her eyelashes at the youngest inspector and made sure she sat next to him while he was writing up a few notes about the activities he had witnessed, while his colleagues were checking the obstacle course. 'Who is the boy with the bandaged wrist?' he asked.

'Gareth Pendragon,' Miranda supplied the necessary information. 'My husband — Philip Hargreaves?' The inflection in her voice suggested everyone had heard of Philip. 'He set up a competition for a boy from a disadvantaged background to enjoy the facilities here for half-term week.'

'Disadvantaged?' the inspector repeated with a frown.

'His mother is a single parent and on a limited budget.'

'I see. And is Gareth enjoying himself?'

'There have been a few issues with my son,' Miranda admitted.

'Your son?'

'Hugo. He's the tall child over there with the swimming party. He is so good with the younger boys. I'm not pointing the finger of accusation at anyone, but after Gareth arrived Hugo's trainers disappeared and I had to buy him some new ones.'

'I see your son's not wearing flotation aids. Have they gone missing too?'

'He isn't actually in the water, is he? Finn's very strict on that sort of thing,' Miranda gushed. 'I know Hugo won't go into the water without them.'

'I understand there was also a fight.'

'That was one of the issues I was telling you about.' Miranda fidgeted on the tree stump. 'Two of the boys came onto Hugo. He didn't stand a chance. I don't have to tell you that one of them was Gareth Pendragon.'

'Is that how Gareth sprained his wrist?'

'No. I believe his school doesn't promote physical activities. He lost his balance on one of the exercises and fell over. It was nothing to do with my son.'

'From what you're saying, it would seem you don't support your husband in this new venture of his, the proposed trust?'

Fearing she may have overstepped the mark, Miranda was quick to reassure the inspector. 'I think it's an excellent idea. I'm updating the website and I'm about to take some photos of young Gareth. His mother has given her permission.'

This last comment wasn't strictly true. Eirlys had not given anything of the sort, but Miranda had never been one to let a minor technicality stand in her way.

'I'd like to speak to Mrs Pendragon. Can you point her out to me?'

'She's the one wearing the flowery summer dress.' Miranda's eyes registered her dissatisfaction as she noticed Eirlys was deep in conversation with Finn. 'Shall I introduce you?'

'Thank you.' The inspector capped his pen. 'But that won't be necessary.' Leaving Miranda still seated on the upturned tree trunk, the inspector made his way over. He approached Eirlys and Finn. 'May I have a word with — Eirlys isn't it? You don't mind me using your first name?'

'I'll leave you to it.' Finn tipped the brim of his ranger's hat and strolled away.

'I understand your son had an accident? Can you tell me what happened?'

'I wasn't here at the time,' Eirlys replied. 'A full report was made out. Have you seen it? I have nothing to add to what's already been said.'

'Good answer.' The inspector smiled. 'And yes, I have read it.'

'Was there anything else?' Eirlys asked, anxious not to spend too long with the authorities in case she inadvertently said the wrong thing.

'Only to ask if you and your son are enjoying your stay here?'

'Very much. It's the experience of a lifetime.'

'And you would recommend the proposed trust scheme?'

'I would.'

A loud barking disturbed the tranquillity of the lakeside scenario, and the next moment a white-haired dog raced out of the trees and began running round in circles, upsetting the various projects the boys had been displaying to the inspectors. In the ensuing chaos Eirlys noticed Hugo lounging by a tree with the suggestion of a smirk on his face. He made no attempt to capture the dog. The animal was delighted by this new game of chasing the boys and was doing everything in her power to escape being caught.

'For heaven's sake, Dixie,' Finn said. Eirlys didn't think she had ever seen him so annoyed. 'What were you thinking of?' he thundered at her as Dean and a couple of the older boys finally managed to restrain the overexcited animal. 'This is Polly, isn't it?'

'Yes,' she answered in a voice that was barely above a whisper.

'You know the rules. No dogs allowed on the site.'

'I know, but I couldn't ask my mother to cancel her holiday. The hotel she's staying at doesn't take dogs. There was nowhere else she could go, and I couldn't afford the kennels. I made sure she had plenty of water, and the cabin door was secured.' Eirlys could see Dixie was doing her best to fight down her tears.

'You mean she was in your quarters?'

'She must have managed to escape.'

'Who else knew about this?' Finn demanded.

'I did.' Dean came forward. 'There was no way Polly could have got out,' he insisted. 'I double-checked.'

'Perhaps someone could return the animal to its billet?' the inspector intervened.

A silence descended on the group as Dixie scooped up the Labradoodle and, cradling the dog in her arms, headed back towards the cabins.

'I think our inspections are complete. Thank you for your hospitality, Finn. If I may have a private word, perhaps in your office?' The senior inspector addressed him.

★ ★ ★

116

The mood around the campfire that evening after the boys had gone to bed was not upbeat. Rumours were rife and were immediately contradicted by counter-rumours about what was going to happen to the camp. No one seemed to have any enthusiasm for the usual evening activities. There was no sign of Dean or Dixie, and Finn had been holed up in his office for hours after the inspectors had left. He hadn't taken any supper and everyone was growing restless.

'Does anyone know anything?' Eirlys asked Hannah, who had joined them after the supper things had been cleared away and the boys were in their cabins.

'It's not official, but I believe Dean and Dixie have been asked to leave.'

'It wasn't Dixie's fault; Polly escaped.'

'She broke the rules, and you know how strict Finn is on that sort of thing.'

'But can't he look at the bigger picture? Dixie's marvellous with the boys. Gareth thinks she's wonderful, and it's not as if Polly did any harm.'

'I agree with you, but the decision

doesn't lie with me,' Hannah replied. 'But I do wish something would happen. All this waiting around is getting on my nerves.'

A disturbance in the distance caught the corner of Eirlys' eye.

'It's Finn,' one of the rangers announced.

'And Miranda's with him,' someone else remarked.

Eirlys decided to stay put by the campfire. Although she wasn't a member of staff, like everyone else she wanted to know what they had decided.

'If I could have your attention please.' Finn raised his voice, although there was no need. Everyone had fallen silent, anxious to hear what he had to say. Miranda positioned herself firmly by Finn's side. Her body language indicated she was there to stay. She nudged Finn and nodded in Eirlys' direction, but Finn appeared not to notice her presence.

'I'm sure you are all aware of today's events down by the lake during the inspectors' visit,' he began, 'so there's no need for me to go into further detail on that.'

'What's happened to Dean?' one of the young male rangers enquired.

'I have asked both him and Dixie to leave with immediate effect.'

The uproar was instantaneous.

'That's not fair.'

'You can't do that.'

'Finn can do whatever he likes,' Miranda raised her voice above the hubbub.

'Why don't we wait to hear what else Finn has to say,' Hannah put in, 'before interrupting.'

Finn threw her a grateful look. 'Thank you, Hannah. The inspectors have informed me that if there are any more transgressions or unfortunate incidents similar to the ones we have already experienced, the camp will be summarily closed down.'

One or two people looked as though they would like to interrupt, but were immediately shushed by their neighbours.

'They liked what they saw and approved of the general atmosphere of the camp. What they have suggested is that we stage an open day where the public can visit. The inspectors could then mingle with the visitors in more casual surroundings to reassure themselves that we run a tight ship.'

'That's a good idea,' Nurse Jackie approved.

'If we can get it together,' Miranda advised.

'Mrs Hargreaves,' Finn continued, 'has contacted her husband. He has promised to do all he can to help and will be paying a visit to the camp as soon as he can. He is open to comments and suggestions from you all, so if you have any issues you can raise them with him. Now, questions?'

'Couldn't Dixie and Dean be given a second chance?' a plea went up from one of the laundry assistants.

Eirlys raised her hand, not caring that she wasn't on the strength. 'How about a written warning on their files?'

'You can't let them leave. They've worked so hard to help get this place on its feet,' someone else put in.

'And they've put in loads of extra hours.'

To Eirlys' surprise, Miranda joined in the cause. 'It would unsettle the children, Finn,' she said, 'if both of them were to leave. And right now we don't have trained replacements. It would increase the workload on the others, and we don't want any more accidents.'

'I can't have a breach of the rules.'

'Just this once?' Miranda coaxed. 'How about if they pay some sort of fine?'

'Polly cannot stay.'

Sensing he was weakening, Miranda pushed home her advantage. 'Of course not. I'm sure arrangements can be made. I could always take the dog home for a few days while Dixie sorts something out.'

'I'll speak to the pair of them,' Finn conceded, 'but I'm not making any promises.'

'Eirlys gets on very well with Dean, don't you? I'm sure she would be pleased to help look after him. You know, stop him straying from the straight and narrow?'

Caught unawares by Miranda's question, Eirlys realised she should have seen something of this nature coming. Finn raised his eyebrows in her direction.

Eirlys stood up. 'I'm still on laundry duty and I wouldn't want to transgress the rules. If you'll excuse me.' Hoping her parting shot had been sufficiently dignified, she made her way back to where the towels were still airing on a makeshift line. Annoyed with herself for beginning to half-like Miranda, she unpegged the towels and carried them back inside.

9

When Finn proposed an evening barbecue the next day and posted the details on the notice board, everyone had been eager to fall in with his suggestion. After being given an official warning, both Dixie and Dean had been allowed to stay on with the understanding there were to be no further incidents. They had both agreed to this condition and had been reinstated.

With everyone eager to get the running of the camp back onto an even keel, volunteers gathered by the lakeside while Eirlys and several of the kitchen assistants cooked mountains of sausages, melted butter over corn on the cob, and roasted baked potatoes on the campfire. An impromptu game of rounders broke out, and the clack of the bat on the ball and high-pitched laughter rang through the forest.

'Something smells good. Need any help?' Finn asked. 'I can wield a mean roasting fork.'

'We can manage, thanks,' one of the assistants said, smiling back at him. 'Hope you're hungry,' she added.

'I think maybe I could manage a sausage or two,' Finn replied.

Eirlys had moved away from the conversation. Ever since Miranda's innuendos about her relationship with Dean, she had no wish to fuel further rumours of any nature. If Miranda took it into her head to go public with her suspicions that there was the faintest link of an attraction between herself and Finn, the future of the camp could be placed in further jeopardy, and Eirlys wanted no part in any nonsense of that nature.

Finn, it appeared, did not harbour the same reservations. 'I don't see Gareth here,' he said with his usual easy smile as he strolled over to speak to her.

'He felt tired,' Eirlys admitted, surprised that her son had opted out of the barbecue. Hugo had offered to stay behind to keep him company — something that would have caused Eirlys a bout of anxiety had Dixie not promised to keep an eye on them.

'For the moment I'm maintaining a low profile,' she had explained to Eirlys, 'so I'll give the barbecue a miss too. By the way, thanks for sticking up for me.'

'I didn't really do anything,' Eirlys insisted.

'Thanks anyway.' Dixie smiled.

'I think you should know Miranda's been implying things about me and Dean.'

'I heard.'

'None of it's true,' Eirlys was quick to put in. 'I mean, I like Dean. He's good with Gareth too. We both like him.'

'You don't have to convince me,' Dixie assured her. 'If you give me your word that what I am about to tell you goes no further . . . ' She paused while Eirlys nodded. ' . . . Dean and I are an item, so I know there's no truth in what Miranda said.'

Bolstered by the welcome news of their relationship and Dixie's promise to keep an eye on Gareth, Eirlys had decided to join the party down by the lake.

'There's going to be music later on,' Finn informed her. 'Of a sort,' he added. 'One of the boys has got a mouth organ and someone else has produced a guitar.'

'Grub's up,' a helper called out, and Finn drew Eirlys to one side to avoid the stampede of hungry boys about to descend on the food.

'Look out, don't want to get crushed in the rush,' Finn warned.

'I'm sorry about what happened yesterday,' Eirlys said.

'You have nothing to apologise for. I read the inspectors' preliminary reports, and they were very complimentary about the proposed trust. They all thought it was an excellent idea, and that Gareth was a good junior ambassador for the scheme.'

'I understand Miranda was making waves.'

'She backed down when she realised the possible repercussions of her actions. If the camp closes Philip might hold her in part responsible. That's why she volunteered to look after Dixie's dog and why she supported the group who wanted to keep Dean and Dixie on.'

'I'm glad they are both staying.'

'I have to admit I'd be lost without them; that's why I was so angry with Dixie. It was a silly thing to do. I don't know what got into her. I'm sorry for my outburst, by the way. I shouldn't have lost my cool in front of everyone.'

'I suppose you had every right to be angry,' Eirlys sympathised. 'You had a lot riding on the inspection.'

'Will you help with the open day?' Finn asked. 'Your business studies would be an invaluable asset in the planning of the occasion.'

'Gareth and I will be long gone by then,' Eirlys replied.

'Surely you'll come back for it? Everyone's got lots of ideas. We had a think tank meeting after breakfast this morning and the guys came up with some pretty outlandish proposals.'

'Wouldn't keeping it simple be a better idea?'

'My thoughts entirely, but I didn't want to douse their enthusiasm, so I told them to devise a chart or something along those lines, to see what they could drum up. I think I could be in for some interesting suggestions.'

The flames from the fire turned his eyes a gentle shade of brown. In the half-light, Eirlys felt more than ever drawn to him. She had tried hard to fight the growing attraction but tonight she sensed Finn felt the same way. Although there had been no one special in her life since Marcus, there was no mistaking the masculine warmth in Finn's eyes.

'I presume Miranda will want to be involved,' Eirlys said, determined to keep introducing her name into the conversation, if nothing else to remind Finn that as the other woman she was always in the background.

'It will be difficult to keep her away,' Finn admitted. 'She is Philip's wife and he is my main investor.'

'Does Philip know what happened yesterday?'

'I updated him. He didn't seem too perturbed and did his best to reassure us it was a storm in a teacup.' His lips curled in a rueful smile. 'I was rather wound up, to say the least.'

'You'd best get in the queue,' Hannah shouted over, waving her fork at them. 'The food is disappearing quicker than snow in the desert. Relish is over there, young man,' she said. 'Now move along; you're holding everyone up.'

'Hannah's in her element. Cooking and bossing people about are her two favourite pastimes,' Finn said with an indulgent look in her direction.

'I suppose we had better join the end of the queue if we want to get anything to eat tonight,' Eirlys said.

'Despite Hannah's concern, I think there's more than enough to go round.

As usual, she's catered for a small army. Have you seen the pile of doughnuts on the go? How she had time to make them with everything else that's been going on, I have no idea.'

'You're lucky to have such a loyal team.'

'That's why I'm so keen for the open day to attract lots of visitors and for it to be a success.' He turned his head as one of the smaller boys struggled past them carrying a loaded plate. 'Good grief, have you seen how many sausages he's got?'

'Perhaps we ought to get a move on,' Eirlys laughed. 'With this lot of gannets, supplies might run low.'

'I hope they don't,' Finn muttered. 'I don't want another mutiny on my hands, to add to all our recent troubles.'

One of the helpers began to play a tune on his mouth organ, and those of the boys who had finished eating began to play air guitar along to the music.

Finn sat down beside Eirlys on the grass and began to gnaw on a chunk of homemade bread. 'What are they doing?' he asked.

'It's simulation hip-hop garage,' Eirlys replied.

'It's what?' Finn looked completely baffled.

'Never mind, just sit back and feel old.'

The evening passed in a happy mixture of warmth, songs, good food and laughter. It was as if the dramas of the previous day had never happened. To Eirlys' surprise, when pressed into a solo by the guitar-playing student, Finn proved to be a fine tenor. As his voice soared high into the night air, several people joined in the chorus, and Eirlys fought down emotions she had no right to feel and even less right to express.

With the memory of the intimate scene she had witnessed between Finn and Miranda on the day of her arrival at the camp, it was vital she overcome moments of weakness such as she was experiencing now. Her presence here was dictated solely by the fact that she was the mother of a young son. Finn would not reciprocate her feelings. He was a professional doing his job and emotional complications were not on the agenda.

Glad they would soon be going home, Eirlys stacked plates as the boys began to yawn; and despite protestations that they wanted to stay up longer, they were now firmly in Nurse Jackie's charge, as she insisted they return to their cabins. A chattering crocodile of youngsters followed her up the path, back to the camp. Night noises from the river intermingled with the rustle of bin liners as litter was collected and the male rangers dismantled the makeshift tables.

'I suppose you don't fancy a night cap in the office?' Finn suggested. 'I've always got some tea on the go, or there's hot chocolate if you prefer.'

Eirlys, who had been feeling as sleepy as the boys, was now wide awake. 'I'm on breakfast duty in the morning, so I've got an early start.'

Finn glanced at his watch. 'It isn't that late. One cup of tea won't hurt.'

Unable to think of a good reason to refuse, Eirlys agreed. 'A hot drink would finish off the evening.'

They followed the shadowy figures drifting up the path to the main camp. Snippets of conversation floated back down to them, amid bouts of happy laughter.

'I'd say the evening was a success, wouldn't you?' Finn enquired. 'Careful.' He grabbed her hand to steady her as yet again she tripped over a protruding tree stump. With their fingers entwined, they climbed the rest of the way. Eirlys hoped that in the gloom no one else would notice the physical intimacy.

'Night, Finn,' several voices called out of the darkness. 'See you tomorrow, Eirlys.'

Finn fumbled in the darkness for the office keys. 'Where's a decent security light when you want one?' he grumbled after several unsuccessful attempts to insert the correct key into the lock. 'Ah, that's it.' He flicked on the switch, bathing the room in a garish yellow glow. They both blinked as their eyes adjusted from the darkness to artificial light. 'Careful you don't lose your footing. I never seem to have enough room,' Finn warned as he made his way around a stack of files. 'Paperwork isn't one of my strengths,' he said. 'Now, where are we?' He rummaged through the debris and came up with two mugs. 'It's a start,' he announced.

'Want me to make the tea?' Eirlys offered. 'Or would you prefer hot chocolate?'

'You know how to make both?'

'I have made buckets of hot chocolate in my time. Small boys drink it by the gallon, especially after football practice.'

Finn waved the kettle at her. 'In that case, the stage is all yours. I'll see if I can unearth the biscuits. I'm sure there's a tin around somewhere.'

They busied themselves with their chores for several minutes, working in companionable silence.

Eirlys stirred the chocolate into the mugs. 'It's ready.'

Finn inspected the festive tin. 'Here we are, a present from some grateful parents. Better put these out for tea tomorrow. We're getting alarmingly near the best-before date. I should have produced them earlier, but to be honest I forgot where I'd put them. What do you fancy, a ginger nut or an orange cream?'

Eirlys peered over the selection chart, then jumped out of her skin as the door to the office crashed open.

'I thought I'd find the two of you cosying up together.'

Eirlys bit down a sigh. It seemed forever to be her fate to have Miranda Hargreaves following her every move.

With admirable aplomb Finn greeted her politely. 'Miranda.'

'Hugo made an emergency call. He tells me you didn't invite him to the barbecue down by the lake. Instead he was made to baby-sit Gareth.'

'That's not true,' Eirlys interjected.

Miranda disregarded her reaction as if it was of no importance. 'It's just as well he didn't go anyway.'

'Has something happened?' Finn asked, an edge to his voice.

'You could say that.'

'What?' Finn snapped when she didn't immediately continue.

'Hugo found his trainers and some of the other stuff that was missing.'

'And?' Finn prompted, but Eirlys didn't need any prompting. She knew what Miranda was going to say.

'They were in Gareth's locker,' she pronounced. She stood in the doorway, hands on her hips, looking like a cat about to demolish a saucer of cream.

10

'You don't have to leave,' Finn repeated his plea.

'I think it would be better all round,' Eirlys insisted.

'You can't think I believe Miranda's outrageous suggestions.'

Eirlys tossed her head. 'I don't know what you believe. What's more, I don't really care. What I do care about is my son being branded a thief.'

'I have not branded him a thief.'

Eirlys was breathing so hard it hurt her chest. They were still in Finn's office. He had asked Miranda to leave after she had delivered her bombshell. With a triumphant look on her face she had departed, closing the door very quietly behind her.

'It will be impossible to keep things quiet. Miranda will make sure everyone knows what happened. I can't accuse anyone of anything because the evidence is stacked against me. Philip will support his wife, and I do not intend to stay around to hear my son's integrity ripped to shreds.'

'Why don't you let things cool down a bit before you do anything rash?'

To her annoyance, Eirlys could hear her voice shaking. 'I don't think there's anything more to be said on the subject, do you?'

'Yes I do,' Finn insisted. 'I don't know what happened here, but I am determined to find out — and until I do, you and Gareth are not guilty of anything, and I won't have anyone else saying otherwise.'

Eirlys raised her voice to match Finn's, not caring who overheard their exchange. 'You can't stop them. Besides, it would be useless to point out we won't be guilty of anything after any investigation either, because we didn't do anything.' She battled on, not entirely sure if what she was saying made sense. 'I suppose next you'll be accusing Gareth of fraying that rope on the bridge, as well as hiding the security equipment and the birthday card in his locker.'

'Of course I won't.'

'Why not? He seems to be getting the blame for everything else that's wrong around here.'

'I am not pointing the finger of accusation at anyone.'

'It may have escaped your notice but Miranda is.'

'She spoke without thinking. When everyone's calmed down she'll realise she was being foolish.'

'That's a great weight off my mind. Meanwhile, I'm giving you formal notice. Gareth and I will be leaving in the morning; and in response to your earlier request, we do not want to be involved in your open day, and I would be grateful if you would remove any of our proposed endorsements from your website.' With blurred vision, she fumbled for the door handle and stumbled into a figure hovering outside.

Eirlys did her best to gather her

thoughts. 'Dixie?'

'I'd like to wring his neck,' the young girl hissed.

'Join the queue.' Eirlys found it difficult to speak in a normal voice. 'Finn always sides with Miranda.'

'Not Finn, I'm talking about Hugo. I know it's unprofessional of me, but I'm convinced that boy is behind all this.'

'You heard what went on in there?' Eirlys gestured towards the office.

'I should think half the camp did.'

'Sorry, but I was so mad.'

'Everyone's behind you.'

'It doesn't matter now. Gareth and I are leaving.'

'You can't go.'

'I'm not staying.'

'No one believes Gareth would steal anything.'

'I'm so upset that Miranda is allowed to get away with her accusations. I couldn't stay on.'

'Let me have a word with Finn.'

Eirlys restrained her. 'No. You're in enough trouble as it is. I wouldn't want you to get another warning on my behalf.'

'Well I'm going to break one of the rules tonight, and to hell with the consequences.'

Eirlys began to feel alarmed. 'Don't do anything silly.'

Dixie laughed at the expression on her face. 'I'm not going to throttle Hugo if that's what's worrying you, much as I'd like to. What I've got in mind is that we spend the night together, if you've no objection to sleeping in staff quarters. We both need company, and if Finn objects I'll set Polly on him. She's got a vicious bark when the mood's on her.'

'Hasn't Miranda got Polly?'

'That woman holds all the aces,' Dixie grumbled.

'I need to see Gareth.'

'No need. He and Archie are holding their own.'

'They're not fighting?'

'No, but Archie is busy reminding Hugo how he fared last time they had a set-to. My advice is to leave the boys to sort it out. Let's have a girly night in my cabin.'

Eirlys could see the sense of Dixie's argument. 'I'll get my things. Be with you in five minutes,' she said.

★ ★ ★

The next morning a vicious hammering on the door woke them up. They had talked long into the night, not falling asleep until the sun was painting the sky with deep purple streaks.

Eirlys groaned and stuck her head under her pillow. 'Go away,' she mumbled.

'I think we've been sussed.' Dixie scrambled out of the bed and peered through the small window. 'I don't believe it,' she gasped.

Eirlys emerged from her hiding place. 'Now what?'

'Miranda flippin' Hargreaves, that's what.'

'Doesn't that woman have a home to go to?'

142

Dixie concealed herself behind a curtain and watched Miranda cup her hands and call out, 'Eirlys, I know you're in there.'

'Can't Finn impose some sort of banning order on her?' Eirlys grumbled. 'She's won. I'm going home. What more does she want?'

'I'll deal with this.' Dixie began to scramble into her discarded clothes. 'Don't do anything until I've talked to her.'

The door burst open before Dixie could get to it.

'What on earth's going on?' Dixie demanded as Miranda fell onto the bed.

Miranda fought for breath. 'The boys. It's your fault.'

'We went through all that last night.' Eirlys delivered a hefty shove, but Miranda refused to budge. 'I'm leaving as soon as I can get dressed. So will you please move? There isn't room for you in here.'

'They've gone.'

'Who's gone?' Dixie was now dressed and more in command of the situation.

'Gareth and Hugo.'

'What are you talking about now?' Dixie was unable to keep the annoyance out of her voice. 'More trouble?'

'Archie reported them missing at breakfast.' Miranda took a deep breath. 'Finn's organising a search party.'

'What?' Eirlys shrieked. 'Why didn't anyone tell me?'

'We couldn't find you. There was a rumour doing the rounds that you'd left the camp and taken the boys with you. That's when Finn telephoned me. Then Dean said he thought he might have seen you sneaking in here late last night.'

Eirlys was no longer listening. 'Out of my way. If your son has harmed my Gareth in any way, I won't be responsible for my actions.'

'My son had nothing to do with this,' Miranda began, but Eirlys and Dixie raced out of the cabin, not bothering to listen to her protest.

'Thank goodness you're still here,' came a familiar deep voice. Eirlys was enveloped in a bear hug as she emerged from Dixie's cabin. Finn's shirt smelt of last night's campfire smoke and burnt sausages. Like everyone else, he hadn't had time to change his clothes.

Eirlys thumped him away from her. 'What's going on?'

Finn hadn't shaved and his hair was in need of a comb. 'The boys are missing. Archie and one of the other lads in the cabin only realised when Hugo and Gareth didn't turn up for breakfast. Everyone thought they were in the shower.'

Dean strode over. He had a rope tied around his waist. 'I suggest we try the tumbledown.'

Miranda began to sob. 'I knew it.'

Before she could get any further, Nurse Jackie grabbed her by the shoulders and slapped her cheek.

Miranda hiccupped. 'You struck me.' She put a hand to her face.

'The best thing for hysterics. Now are you going to be of some use, or do I have to sedate you?'

'What? No. I'm going with the rescue party.'

'Then no more nonsense?'

Miranda hesitated, looking as though she might make a scene, before deciding the nurse had the upper hand. She nodded.

'Right, let's be on our way,' Finn said.

Dean looked at his boss. 'OK if I take charge, Finn?'

'You're sure the boys are there?'

'We've searched everywhere else, and Archie says Hugo was daring Gareth to go back to the tumbledown with him.'

'Off we go then.'

'I'm coming with you,' Eirlys insisted.

Miranda fell into step beside her before she could object. 'My son may be in danger too,' she said in a different tone of voice to the one she normally used when speaking to Eirlys.

Eirlys hesitated, then nodded, and the two women began to follow the rescue party. They were five minutes into the forest before one of the helpers called out, 'isn't that Gareth?'

Eirlys ran forward and gathered up her son in her arms. 'Are you all right?' she demanded. 'You're very pale.'

'Hugo,' he gasped.

Miranda pushed her way forward. 'What about him?'

'I'll deal with this.' Eirlys shielded her son from the older woman. 'Why isn't Hugo with you?' she asked in as calm a voice as she could manage.

'He dared me to stand on the floorboards and I did.' Gareth cast a nervous glance in Miranda's direction, then lapsed into silence.

'Go on,' Eirlys prompted.

'I wanted to prove I was as brave as you when you went down the zip wire. Mum, I didn't steal those trainers or the birthday card.'

'Never mind that now,' Eirlys urged. 'Where's Hugo?'

'When it was his turn to stand on the floorboards there was a funny noise, then the wood cracked and he fell through.'

147

'Is he badly injured?' Miranda shrieked.

'I don't think so. He shouted out and I said I was going for help.' Gareth's face crumpled. 'I don't like the tumble-down. It's a horrid place. Am I in trouble?'

'We'll talk about it later.' Eirlys kissed his forehead. 'You've been a very brave boy.'

'I did the dare, didn't I?' he said, seeking approval.

'You did. Now can you do something even more important and show us exactly where Hugo fell?'

The rest of the group trampled through the undergrowth with Eirlys and Gareth in the lead, followed by a sobbing Miranda.

Eirlys gasped at the sight of the wrecked old building, then restrained Gareth as he went to run towards it. 'You went in there?'

'I have to show you where Hugo fell.'

'No. Leave it to Dean.'

'Let me go first,' Nurse Jackie insisted.

'Don't walk on anything,' Finn cautioned her.

'I need to know if the boy is hurt.'

'Quiet, everyone,' Dean called out. 'Hugo?'

'I'm here,' a faint voice rose from inside the tumbledown.

'I'll call the emergency services. Does anyone have a mobile on them?' Jackie looked round.

'They're all back at the camp,' Finn admitted, 'and my two-way radio is on the blink.'

'You and your wretched rules.' Miranda seemed to have found her voice again. 'Eirlys is right. You're a dinosaur.'

'This is not the time for that,' Finn snapped back. 'Jackie, take one of the rangers with you and go back to the camp and make your call.'

'Right away.'

'It could be ages before they get here, Finn,' Dean murmured in his ear. 'What do you suggest we do?'

'Would the boards in the tumbledown take my weight?'

'I doubt it. If Hugo fell in, they wouldn't support a grown man.'

'But they might support a child.' Miranda elbowed her way forward. 'Gareth?'

'My son is going nowhere near that place.' Eirlys was having none of Miranda's suggestion.

'I agree.' Jackie put a restraining hand on Gareth's shoulder. 'With your permission, Eirlys, I'm taking your son back to camp. He's done enough for one day and I need to attend to him in the medical centre.'

Eirlys nodded, and before anyone could object, Jackie and one of the rangers swung round and began to make their way back to base.

'Hugo — won't anyone help him?' Miranda pleaded.

'Finn,' Eirlys said, tugging his sleeve, 'we can't leave him down there. It could be at least an hour before the emergency services arrive.'

'What do you suggest we do?'

'I'm willing to try it.'

'Try what?'

'To rescue him.'

150

'No.'

'I'm the smallest person here. The boards should stand my weight.'

'I can't allow it.'

'If I lie flat and lean down, perhaps Hugo could reach up and grab my arms.'

'It's possible,' Dean intervened, 'if someone held onto Eirlys' legs to stop her going through.'

'I'll do it,' Miranda volunteered.

'Stay away,' Finn ordered in a voice that brooked no disobedience.

'I only want to help.'

'The best thing you can do is stay back. Now, are you sure?' He held Eirlys by the shoulders and looked hard into her eyes.

She looked back at Finn. 'I'm the mother of a young son too. I'd never forgive myself if anything happened to Hugo and I'd done nothing to prevent it.'

'I'll rig up a harness,' Dean suggested, 'similar to the one you wore on the zip wire, Eirlys. You can put it round your middle, then we'll organise a chain of helpers to hold onto each other to stop you falling through. Are you OK with that?'

'I'm fine.'

'Great guy.'

Ten minutes later all was ready.

'Right,' Finn said, testing the harness for strength. 'Are you ready?'

Eirlys nodded. Her heart was beating so loudly she could barely hear what anyone was saying. 'Glad I did the trial run on the zip wire,' she said in a shaky voice.

'Places, everyone,' Dean called out, 'and we need absolute silence.'

Eirlys lay on her stomach and tried to ignore her thumping pulse.

'Right, off you go. Take it steady,' Dean instructed.

Eirlys edged forward. The boards shifted under her as she wriggled along. 'Hugo?' she called out. 'It's Eirlys. Can you hear me?'

'My leg hurts,' he whimpered.

'Can you move it?'

'Yes.'

'And your arms?'

'Yes.'

'Can you see me?'

'Yes, through the crack.'

'Then put your hand up so I can see it. Very good,' Eirlys said as Hugo wiggled his fingers at her.

'Now what?'

'If I come forward and put my arms down the hole, could you grab them?'

'I don't know.'

'Shall we try?'

'Where's my mother?'

'She's here, outside.'

'I want her.'

'Then do as I say and we'll get to see her very soon, won't we?'

'You won't let go?'

'I promise. Can you stand?'

More of Hugo's arm appeared, then the top of his curly head as he struggled to his feet.

'Hello.' Eirlys smiled as he grabbed her arm. 'Now put your hands round my neck.'

'I can't,' he wailed.

'Come on, Hugo,' Dean called out behind Eirlys, 'remember all those keep-fit exercises we did on the obstacle course?'

'Yes.'

'Then show Eirlys how good you are at stretching.'

Two arms were tightened around Eirlys' neck.

'I've got him.' Hugo's jumper muffled her words as she secured her arms around his waist.

'Right, everyone,' Dean called, 'back off. We're coming out. Gently does it.'

Eirlys could feel hands pulling at her legs as she lifted Hugo out of the cellar. The floorboards gave another alarming creak.

'What was that?' Hugo was trembling in her arms.

'Nothing,' Eirlys reassured him.

'One last pull,' Dean ordered.

The next moment Eirlys was rolling on her back on hard ground with a sobbing Hugo still in her arms. Several hands tried to release him, but it was as if they were welded together. Eirlys had no idea how long they stayed like that until she felt a firm pair of hands haul her to her feet. She was no longer clutching Hugo's sobbing body. Instead Finn was holding her, his lips were on hers and she surrendered to her first kiss in over five years.

11

Eirlys swung round at the sound of a tap on the door. 'May I come in?' A tall man ducked his head and attempted to enter the room.

'Who are you?' she demanded as she flung the last of her belongings into her holdall.

'I didn't realise space was so cramped in the guest accommodation. Do you mind if I perch on the end of the bed?'

Eirlys zipped up her bag. 'As you wish.'

'You're leaving?' the man asked.

'I don't wish to appear rude, Mr — ?' Eirlys paused. 'I didn't catch your name.'

'We haven't been introduced have we? Philip Hargreaves.' He held out a hand. Eirlys ignored it. 'Hugo's father,' he added helpfully.

'If you've come to throw the book at me, there's no need. As you were

156

observant enough to notice, I am leaving.'

'Not on my account, I hope.'

Eirlys put her hands on her hips and took a deep breath; but before she could speak, Philip got in first.

'I don't know how to thank you. I've received a garbled report from my wife about you saving my son's life. If it wouldn't delay you too much, and as no one else seems to be able to offer a coherent explanation, could you tell me exactly what happened?'

'I didn't save Hugo's life,' Eirlys insisted.

'That isn't the impression I received. I gather my son is to blame for enticing your boy to this tumbledown place, then after a dare that he instigated he fell through the floorboards, from where you rescued him.'

'That about sums it up.'

'Very rough justice, but I think it has taught Hugo a lesson.'

'How can you say that? Hugo is your son.' Eirlys was outraged that a father could be so dismissive of his child's trauma.

'That came out all wrong, didn't it?' Philip admitted with a rueful smile. 'What I meant to say was, I am not as blind to Hugo's shortcomings as is my wife. I know what an annoying little tyke he can be. I've spoken to Hugo and he's admitted everything — hiding the pilfered goods in Gareth's locker, and generally being a nuisance to all and sundry. I gather he even let a dog loose?'

'Polly. She belongs to one of the staff. The girl was dismissed, but Finn reinstated her and her boyfriend.'

'What a lot of drama I seem to have missed.' Philip smiled. 'Board meetings are very dull in comparison.'

Eirlys acknowledged his words with a reluctant smile. 'Put like that, I suppose a lot has happened.'

'I believe the modern take on Hugo's behaviour is that it was a cry for help.'

'I might call it something else,' Eirlys said, 'but then I seem to be out of tune with everything that goes on here.'

'I'm not attempting to absolve my son in any way,' Philip admitted. 'His behaviour has been appalling. In mitigation, I can only say my wife and I lead busy lives. I've been told you and your son are very close and you are always there for him. To cut a long story short, Hugo was jealous. He's very sorry for the trouble he's caused and assures me it won't happen again.'

Eirlys sat down on the bed beside Philip. 'Thank you,' she said in a tired voice.

'I promise that when my son is fit enough he will personally apologise to you and Gareth. Meanwhile, I hope you'll accept a heartfelt second-hand one through me?'

Eirlys hesitated, then nodded.

'Good.' Philip smiled. 'Now we're friends, will you shake my hand?'

His handshake was firm, and Eirlys found herself warming to the man she had been prepared to dislike on the spot.

'Is there anything I can do to make amends?'

'Does this incident have to be reported to the inspectors?' Eirlys asked.

'I'll speak to them. Don't worry about that.'

'I wouldn't want Gareth being blamed.'

'He won't be.'

Eirlys tossed back her hair. 'I understand the competition was your idea,' she said after a pause.

'Indeed, yes.' Philip warmed to his theme. 'What I have in mind is setting up a fund — a trust. I came from a modest background and I know what it's like to count the pennies. I haven't had time to think everything through yet, but I want other boys from less privileged backgrounds to be able to enjoy all the facilities here. I personally believe it will work. Random reports indicate that Gareth has had a good time.'

'He's been happy,' Eirlys conceded.

'I sense a 'but' coming on.' Philip raised a questioning eyebrow.

'Straight speaking?'

'I wouldn't have it any other way.'

'I don't intend going over old ground, but one way or another Hugo caused a lot of trouble. Finn felt obliged to support Miranda's accusations against my son because she is married to you, his main benefactor.'

'That won't happen again.'

'I can't guarantee that my son's confidence hasn't been dented by his experience here. I am a single parent and he is an only child. We live with my mother-in-law and I make my living by painting from a caravan in the forest. Gareth's background is far removed from that of most of the boys here, and the same could be said for other boys enjoying the benefit of the trust fund. Children can be cruel, and I wouldn't want any youngster to be made to feel inferior.'

'Hm.' Philip looked thoughtful. 'You've made some good points there. Are you saying none of the boys have been friendly?'

'Not at all. Archie, who shares

Gareth's cabin, is a lovely boy; but it only needs a ringleader to stir things up, create peer pressure, and we are back to square one.'

'I take your point.'

'From what Finn tells me, you're not here very often to oversee any changes.'

'That's something else that is going to change,' Philip replied. 'What happened here was a wake-up call. Both Miranda and I have learned a sharp lesson. Our son needs us. If nothing else, Eirlys — may I call you Eirlys?' She nodded. 'You've identified a behavioural pattern in Hugo which I intend to nip in the bud.'

'I'm pleased my stay here was of some use to you. That'll be recompense enough for all that occurred. Now, if you'll excuse me.' She hefted her bag over her shoulder.

'You won't reconsider your decision to leave?'

'My son needs to get back to what's familiar to him.' Eirlys shrugged. 'And I don't feel either of us could stay on after all that's happened. Besides which, I have several commissions on hold, and I can't afford to turn down work.'

'In that case you must allow me to drive you home, and I'm not taking no for an answer,' Philip insisted.

Now all the excitement had died down, the camp appeared to be functioning in an efficient and quiet manner. Dean was putting a group of boys through their fitness paces, and fragrant cooking aromas billowed out from the direction of the kitchen.

'Do you want to make your goodbyes to anyone?' Philip asked.

'Perhaps it might be better if we slipped away without any fuss,' Eirlys suggested.

'As you wish. You fetch Gareth. I'll be in the car park.'

Gareth was sitting on his bunk bed, idly swinging his legs backwards and forwards.

Eirlys greeted him with a cheerful smile. 'Ready?'

Gareth stood up. 'Archie wants to say goodbye.'

A small figure flung his arms around Eirlys' neck. 'Can I come and stay in your caravan?' he asked breathlessly.

'It isn't really suitable for overnight guests.' Eirlys looked into his crestfallen face. 'Perhaps you'd like to come to tea instead one day?'

'Wizard.' The two boys danced a jig.

'Bet my mud slide will be better than yours,' Gareth called over his shoulder as he waved goodbye to his friend.

'What mud slide?' Eirlys asked, intrigued.

'At the open day.' Gareth gave her the long-suffering look little boys give their mothers when they don't pay attention to important issues.

Eirlys did her best to let him down gently. 'I'm not sure we'll be coming back for that.'

'We have to.' Gareth widened his eyes as if that were an end to the matter. 'I'm team leader.'

Without warning, another pair of

arms were flung round Eirlys' neck. She lost her footing and bumped into the body pressed against hers, inhaling a healthy lungful of French perfume.

'I don't know what I would have done if I'd lost my son,' Miranda sobbed into her ear. 'From the bottom of my heart, thank you.' To Eirlys' further discomfort, Miranda planted a kiss on her cheek. She struggled free from the embrace.

'That's all right,' she stuttered.

'Philip tells me you're leaving, and that he's giving you a lift home.'

'If that's not a problem?' Eirlys asked in a guarded voice, unsure how to deal with this new Miranda.

'You'll be back for the open day?'

'Yes,' Gareth assured her. 'I'm team leader.'

'Wonderful.' Miranda beamed at them. 'Hugo is so looking forward to being part of the mud slide gang.' She now gave a tinkling laugh. 'I dread to think of the laundry bill afterwards, but we have to do these things, don't we?'

She glanced at her watch. 'Best go. I'm due to have coffee with Nurse Jackie.'

'Are you?' was all Eirlys could say.

Miranda pulled a face. 'I know. I'm doing my best to behave like a model patient, or rather the mother of a patient, but Jackie can be a dragon, can't she? You know my face still stings from where she slapped me?'

'How is Hugo?' Eirlys managed to get a word in edgewise.

'He had a good night's sleep and is demanding to get up. Jackie is insisting he stay in bed for the morning. That's why I'm going over for coffee, to try to calm things down. I think I might have my hands full.' She waved her manicured nails in their direction. 'Keep in touch,' she insisted.

Gareth tugging her hand dragged Eirlys back to the present. She had been wondering if she had dreamed the whole scene. Was Miranda really promising to keep in touch?

'It's Finn, Mum.' He was striding toward them, looking anxious.

'Why don't you go and say goodbye to the rest of your teammates?' Eirlys suggested to Gareth, who promptly raced off in the direction of the keep-fit team, who were now jogging on the spot.

'How are you feeling?' Finn asked.

After the rescue, Jackie had insisted on giving Eirlys a medical check-up, but apart from a few scratches she had suffered no lasting injury. The only part of her body that was bruised was her lips from when Finn had kissed her.

'Fine.' Her voice was as casual as she could manage.

'Jackie tells me you wouldn't sleep over in the medical unit.'

'Hugo and Miranda needed beds, and there was no need for me to be there.'

'I don't think you should leave.' He eyed her up and down. 'Shock can take a while to set in.'

'Philip has already taken my things to the car.'

'Philip?'

'He's giving us a lift home.'

'I can do that.'

'I wouldn't want to take you away from your camp duties.'

'When will you be coming back?'

'I don't know.'

'Dean has appointed Gareth as one of the team leaders at the open day.'

Eirlys began to feel annoyed. 'I'm not sure I approve of my son being used as blackmail.'

'I know we should have consulted you first,' Finn began to apologise.

'Yes you should,' Eirlys agreed.

'And what happened here was reprehensible, but everyone is trying to put things right. We all want to move on.'

'I agree, and that is why Gareth and I are leaving. We're moving on.'

'I couldn't offer you a job here?'

For the second time in as many minutes, Eirlys stumbled. 'A job? Doing what?'

'You'd be a great asset.'

'You're not serious?'

'Deadly serious. We need more female members of staff. Several of the parents have asked about admitting girls. Obviously the facilities would have to be converted. There would be a lot to do.'

Gareth raced back and began to swing on Eirlys' arms. 'Are we ready to go? And when can Archie come to tea? Hello Finn. I'm team leader at the open day.'

'Well done.' Finn smiled down at him. 'I'm trying to persuade your mother to come and work with us.'

'Brilliant.'

Eirlys glared at Finn. 'You had no right to say that,' she hissed.

'The idea seems to be going down well with your son.'

'I will not have you organising my life. Now I really must go. Philip will be wondering what's happened to me.'

'Eirlys . . . ' Finn lowered his voice and fell into step beside her. 'Please?'

She turned her head swiftly. 'Please what?' The look in his eyes almost had her stumbling yet again. He put out a hand to steady her.

'What you thought you saw that first day, between Miranda and myself?'

'I know exactly what I saw.'

'No you don't. Miranda is a highly emotional woman. She needs constant stimulation. With Philip away, she was always looking for another outlet. Does that make sense?'

'None at all.'

'She imagined an attraction between us. We worked together a lot and I fear she misread the situation.'

They were now approaching the car park.

'Finn, you're telling me things I don't want to hear.'

'Then let me tell you this.'

'There's Philip.' Eirlys waved at him and Gareth ran over, full of admiration for his silver-grey saloon.

'Please come back. I need you.'

'Finn, I can't deal with this. Right now I need to get home.'

Unable to think clearly, Eirlys turned on her heel and headed towards Philip and her son.

12

'Where would you like me to drop you off?' Philip enquired after they had completed most of their journey in near silence.

Eirlys came to her senses with a start. 'I'm sorry,' she apologised.

'I could see you were thinking about other things.'

'I should have telephoned Granny Marcus.'

'Who?' Philip looked baffled.

Eirlys glanced over her shoulder. Exhausted by recent events, Gareth had fallen asleep in the back seat.

'My mother-in-law. That's what Gareth calls her.'

'Right.' Philip's smile was still a tad on the puzzled side.

'I didn't let her know of our change in plans. I'll probably sleep over at the caravan tonight. I have to sort things out, but Gareth needs a change of clothes, a proper bath, that sort of thing.'

'A routine he gets from his grandmother?'

Eirlys nodded, a flush of embarrassment working its way up her neck. She hated having to justify her way of life to strangers.

'The arrangement works well for us,' she said quietly.

'Why don't we see if Granny Marcus is in?' Philip suggested in a kind voice. 'Then after Gareth is settled I can drive you back to the caravan.'

'You've done enough.'

'I've only an empty house to go back to, with Miranda sleeping over at the camp. Please don't turn down my offer.'

'Then you must let me treat you to dinner. Beans on toast?' Eirlys suggested.

'Great idea.'

'It's number seventy-three.' Eirlys indicated Martha Pendragon's bungalow.

Philip drew up outside. 'I'll wait here.'

The front door opened and Gareth, now fully awake, raced down the drive, full of stories about his adventures at the camp. A few moments later Eirlys emerged, clutching a box full of supplies.

'We've enough tins of beans for a feast,' she said as she did up her seat belt. 'I don't know about you, but I'm starving.'

'Did you get any breakfast?'

'I don't think I did,' she admitted.

'And we missed out on lunch, unless you count that bag of crisps we shared in the service station.'

She smiled at him. 'It has been a strange day, hasn't it?'

'One of the best,' Philip insisted. 'Now, where am I going?'

★ ★ ★

'Don't forget to close the gate,' Eirlys said as they stopped in front of her green-painted caravan. 'Philip?' she prompted when he didn't immediately respond.

'You live here?' His voice reflected his surprise.

'Not all the time,' she replied, ready to defend her beloved home, 'but I love it.'

'So do I. What was that about closing a gate?'

'Rules of the countryside.'

Philip saluted. 'On my way.'

Eirlys watched him trudge back to the entrance to the field. His shoes were designer, as were his chinos and sweatshirt, but he didn't seem to mind getting them dirty. She grinned as he struggled to pull the gatepost out of the mud, almost toppling over as it finally came free with a loud sucking noise. Philip made a face as he saw the stains on his trousers. 'Don't you dare laugh,' he ordered with a mock frown.

'I should hurry up if I were you,' Eirlys warned him.

'What? Why?'

'A herd of cows is heading your way, and you won't half get it from Jack if they get out onto the road. It's his herd.'

'Oh my goodness.' Philip leapt into

action as the full impact of his predicament became obvious. The next moment he was surrounded by an inquisitive group of cows, all anxious to see who this newcomer was. Eirlys was now doubled up with laughter as gentle noses butted Philip, flattening him against the gate bars, nuzzling his neck and leaving a trail of warm moisture down the pristine cotton logo of his sweatshirt.

'Will you leave off?' Philip tried to rid himself of the nosiest of the group, a cow who seemed to be doing her best to prevent him from engaging the gate catch.

'Leave you to it,' Eirlys called over. 'Can you bring the supplies in from the car?'

After hearing a muffled oath of assent from somewhere inside the ring of cows, she began to search round for the key to her padlock. She didn't like securing her belongings in this manner, and Jack had insisted it wasn't necessary, but the insurance company had stipulated it was a condition of her policy in order to prevent heavy premiums. Most of her work and supplies were stored in the caravan, and she saw the sense of their argument.

Although it had only been a few days since she and Brian Jackson had paid a visit, the interior smelt musty. Eirlys undid the small window catches to let in a draught of late-afternoon air.

Philip poked a dishevelled head through the door. 'Where do you want these?' He was holding the tins of baked beans.

'Anywhere you can find space. We're going to have to eat outside, if that's all right with you.'

'It's a lovely evening. What can I do to help?'

'You can raise the awning and sort out seating and the table.' A smile spread across her face. 'You might also want to freshen up.' She gestured towards the stains on Philip's shirt. 'You can fill the kettle at the same time if you like, from the clearwater stream.

Here's a towel.' She tossed it at Philip, who caught it with one hand.

'I don't know why you bothered to book into Finn's Forest for a week. You've got all the natural facilities you need right here. Back in a jiffy.'

By the time he returned, the beans were bubbling on the camping stove that Eirlys liked to use.

Philip gave an appreciative sniff. 'Something smells good.'

'Nearly ready. Take a seat.' Eirlys waved her spoon at him.

'Is this thing safe?' He lowered his tall frame into one of the camping seats.

'I haven't lost anyone yet,' Eirlys replied, 'but I wouldn't fidget too much if I were you. It can be a bit temperamental.'

Philip did his best to shuffle the seat up to the table.

Eirlys served up their supper. 'Tuck in. Don't stand on ceremony.'

Steam rose from the two plates and Philip did as he was told.

'Can you manage a banana?' she

asked as he finished demolishing his mountain of baked beans.

'I ought to say no after that healthy portion of beans,' he admitted ruefully, 'but I actually think I could.'

'Me too.'

Eirlys unearthed the fruit from Martha's box of supplies.

'Cheers,' Philip toasted her with his banana. 'You know, I've travelled the four corners of the globe and eaten in some pretty swanky places, but that meal and these surroundings top the lot.'

'It's not quite so user-friendly in the middle of winter,' Eirlys replied, 'when the wind's howling round and there's snow in the air.'

'All the same, it's my sort of place. Reminds me of my holidays when I was a child. I came from a one-parent family too. Things were a struggle when I was growing up. My mother often went without.'

'I took you for a college boy,' Eirlys said in surprise.

'Night school to get my exams. Then hard graft, and years of apprenticeship before I landed the job I love. In many ways I've been lucky, but I've never forgotten my roots.'

In the distance the cows lowed as an evening mist descended on the field.

'Are you sure you won't reconsider your decision about returning to Finn's Forest?' Philip asked.

Eirlys dropped the banana skins into an old bucket. 'Finn wants me to return.'

'I know. He ran the idea past me.'

'I'm flattered, but I can't do it.'

'Why not?'

'Here I have my independence. I decided a long time ago that I would live my life on my terms.'

'You can't shut out the rest of the world.'

'I'm not trying to, but if I accept Finn's offer I'll be beholden to him.'

'And me?'

Eirlys frowned. 'I don't follow.'

'I've put quite an investment into Finn's Forest.'

She nodded. 'Yes.'

'We have plans to expand.'

'I know that too.'

'I intend being more hands-on, but I do require reliable back-up, and you're exactly the sort of person I had in mind.'

'I still don't follow.'

'With your input, we could cater for a broader spectrum of needs.'

'What does that mean?'

'Children relate to you. Young Archie, for instance. It's a rare gift you have, Eirlys. Youngsters need to feel that those in authority aren't against them.'

'I've not got any experience or qualifications.'

'You're a natural, and you wouldn't have to worry about leading an independent lifestyle. You could come back to the caravan as often as you like.'

'There must be far better people able to do the job.'

'You understand a child's psyche, and that's nothing a degree can teach you.'

'I still don't know what you're talking

about,' Eirlys replied, 'but I have a question for you.'

'Go on,' Philip urged.

'Why are you so keen to lure me back to Finn's Forest?'

'I heard about your experience on the zip wire.'

Eirlys pondered on his reply. 'What has that to do with anything?'

'I thought if we introduced a co-ed theme to the camp, you would be the ideal person to nurture the girls. I'm sure you would be able to help them overcome any fears they might have.'

'You seem to forget I'm the mother of a young son. Gareth's needs would have to come first. He couldn't live at the camp all the time, and it would be too far for him to travel on a regular basis.'

'That's something we would need to go into in more depth. But why don't you give it a trial?'

Eirlys shook her head. 'Finn and I wouldn't work well together.'

'How do you know?'

181

Eirlys hesitated. 'We just wouldn't.'

'That's a great pity.' Philip wasn't smiling anymore. 'I was so convinced you would want to help. Finn thought so too.'

'You've discussed it with him?'

'Not in any detail.' He narrowed his eyes in thought.

'I'm sorry to disappoint you.'

'To put it on the line, Eirlys, if we don't get help then I don't think Finn will be able to continue.'

The field lapsed into silence. The evening noises around them stilled as Eirlys absorbed the full meaning of his words. 'If I didn't know better, Philip, I'd say you were using undue influence.'

'That's not my intention, but I suppose I am guilty of exerting a little pressure,' he admitted.

'I still can't understand why you think I'm right for this assignment.'

'Years of experience with people have taught me who's right for a certain project and who's wrong. You are so right for the forest, and for Finn.'

'Is this an elaborate attempt to distract Miranda?'

'Now it's me who's not following you.'

'You can't have failed to notice the attraction between Finn and Miranda.'

From the expression on Philip's face, Eirlys feared she might have over-stepped the mark.

'I agree that Miranda does need a constant stimulus. That's why I'm going to be based at home for the foreseeable future. So in answer to your question, no it isn't.'

Eirlys' supper churned in her stomach. Philip was an expert at bending people to his will. That was why he ran his own highly successful electronics company. He was ambitious and he didn't let people stand in his way. She had been foolish to accept his offer of a lift. She was now in his debt.

'What about Dixie?' she suggested.

'The young girl with the dog?' Philip looked surprised.

'She would be a good choice for the new project.'

'For a start she's too young, and the business with the dog proves she isn't ready for responsibility.'

'Neither am I,' Eirlys was quick to point out. 'I couldn't adapt to Finn's rules and regulations. I even had a go at him about no mobile phones being allowed on site. It was like talking to a brick wall.'

'If you don't like Finn's rules you can make up some of your own.' He leaned forward. 'Don't you see you're turning down the chance of a lifetime?'

A disturbance at the far end of the field caught Eirlys' attention. The rooks rose out of the trees, circling and cawing above them.

'We've got visitors.' Eirlys was pleased to have a distraction. Philip turned round. 'It's probably the farmhands come to round up the cows to take them back to the milking shed for the night,' she said. 'I'll go and let them in.'

'Let me.' Philip leapt to his feet,

leaving Eirlys to clear the table of the remains of their supper.

It was growing dark and, although she could hear the murmur of voices, she couldn't see who Philip was speaking to. Jack's four-by-four bumped over the ruts and he waved at Eirlys. She waved back, then peered into the fading light. Another shadow by the gate moved and a second vehicle drove in. A female laugh rang out. With a sinking heart, Eirlys recognised it immediately. It was Miranda, and the driver behind the wheel of the second vehicle was Finn.

He leapt out and raised his weather-beaten hat. 'Any coffee on the go?' he asked.

13

Philip drove off with Miranda in the passenger seat blowing kisses out of the window. 'Bye, darlings,' she trilled at them. 'Have fun.'

'Coffee?' Finn prompted.

'I still don't understand what's going on.' Eirlys frowned in confusion.

Finn's eyes softened. 'I'll make the coffee. You look as though you could do with a sit-down.'

He was back a few moments later. 'Hannah sent over some of her cookies to sustain us.' He retrieved the plastic container from the four-by-four, then eased his long frame into the seat Philip had recently vacated and undid the cellophane wrapping. Eirlys took one with an absent-minded smile, then watched Finn take a large bite out of his. The coffee was warm and revived her flagging spirits.

'I suppose I do owe you an explanation.' He helped himself to a second biscuit. 'After you left the camp, Miranda collared me. I was trying to get on with my day. Hugo's recovering nicely and she was at a loose end. She was full of ideas for this open day thing, and quite frankly she was getting on my nerves.'

'If this is an attempt to get sympathy . . . ' Eirlys began.

'It isn't,' Finn assured her. 'Where was I?'

'Miranda was getting on your nerves. That must be a first,' she couldn't resist adding.

Finn's smile caused Eirlys' heart to flip and beat faster. She had no right to trust or like this man. He had taken Miranda's side in everything, even allowing her to accuse Gareth of being a thief.

'I was trying to get my head round the forms the inspectors had foisted on me, and several of the guys wanted a meeting about the open day. You'd walked out on me. I had enough on my plate without Miranda bleating on.'

'What was she bleating about?' Eirlys asked, determinedly ignoring his comment about her desertion.

'When I began to pay attention I realised she was offering me a get-out clause.'

'A get-out clause?' Eirlys sat up straight.

'Philip has suggested they take a short holiday.'

'And?'

'She wants Hugo to stay over at the camp while they're away.'

'How does this concern me?'

'She ran it past her son and he was agreeable to the suggestion, if Gareth returned.'

Eirlys spilt coffee over the grass.

'She's willing to pay all costs.'

'Why?'

'Hugo's a changed child. He really wants to be friends with Gareth and he thinks the sun shines out of your eyes. Although I would never have wished such a fate on the boy, falling through those floorboards changed him. I don't know how; perhaps he banged his head or something.' He looked at her expectantly.

'There's no way I am going to be in debt to Miranda Hargreaves. And even if I agreed to her scheme, I couldn't afford to pay for Gareth staying over at the camp.'

'I thought you might say that, so I have another suggestion. How about if you come to help with the open day after Gareth's broken up from school?' he suggested. 'That should give you enough time to arrange things. And as you'd technically be a member of staff, there would be no expenses involved. I'm sure Miranda could work round that.'

'Is everyone ganging up on me?' Eirlys demanded.

'Yes.'

'Philip tried to — what did you say?'

'Yes.'

'Then I'll give you the same answer I

gave Philip. I have commissions to complete,' she insisted, 'and Gareth has had enough disruption in his life recently — a fact that everyone has overlooked.'

Finn banged the picnic table with his knee as he leaned forward and put out a hand to clasp Eirlys'. He squeezed her fingers. It was as if the movement set off a buzzer in her head.

'Eirlys, I want to make things up to you. We all do.'

'I keep telling you, Finn. I have my own life. I don't want to be an extension of yours.'

An expression Eirlys didn't understand flickered across Finn's face. 'I'm not good at putting my feelings into words,' he said.

She was doing her best to convince herself that the noise in her ears was from farm vehicles in the far field and nothing to do with the tangled emotions befuddling her brain.

'We got off on the wrong foot. I know that. I just couldn't believe that someone like you would one day walk into my life when I was least expecting it. I've always been a loner — working with nature, you get used to being on your own — so I don't have much experience of personal relationships.'

'Don't go on,' Eirlys implored.

He brushed aside her objection. 'I have to.'

'Why?' she asked. 'Why now?'

'Because I could see I was in danger of losing you forever.'

'I don't know what to say,' Eirlys admitted.

'You wouldn't be giving up your independence. You could have your own space.'

Eirlys snatched her hand out of his grasp. 'I can't take all this in.'

'Please say you'll think about it. Everyone's been bending my ear at the camp, saying I'd behaved like a pig-headed fool over the Miranda and Hugo business.'

A reluctant smile curved Eirlys' mouth. 'You won't get any sweet words from me either.'

Finn's look of outrage deepened.

'Yes, I understand you've been stirring things up too.'

'Whatever do you mean?'

'Dean tells me you want to rewrite some of my rules.'

'Some of them are plain silly.'

'I beg your pardon?' He now looked affronted.

'That one about mobile phones for a start.'

'I banned them on site because the boys spent their days downloading apps and games.'

'Fair enough, but there was no need to ban them wholesale. They have their uses, especially in emergencies, as you know only too well.'

'Let's not go into all that now,' Finn backtracked. 'What I really want to know is, will you consider my suggestion?'

'I'm not exactly sure what it was.'

'Will you help with the organisation of the open day? Deep down you know Gareth would love to live on site while you do. It's quite comfortable, really. His role as team leader should boost his confidence. What do you think?'

'And after the open day is over?'

'One step at a time?' Finn suggested.

'There's Gareth's grandmother to consider.'

'Martha, isn't it? Granny Marcus?' Eirlys nodded. 'She can come and visit any time she likes.'

'I'm sure she would insist on it. Apart from Gareth, she's the only relation I have in the world. By the way, I should warn you she's feisty. She comes from a fishing background, and if she doesn't like you then you are history.'

An uneasy look crossed Finn's face. 'Perhaps we won't invite her over just yet,' he amended his offer.

'Yes we will,' Eirlys insisted.

'Does that mean we're on?' He looked hopeful again.

'I didn't say that,' she was quick to intercede.

'But you're not turning me down out of hand?'

'I'm promising nothing.'

'I know it's a lot to ask.'

193

He leaned back in his canvas chair and closed his eyes. Eirlys noticed the dark circles under them. He looked as though he'd lost weight too, and his hair was badly in need of a trim. A few moments later he was breathing deeply.

Trying not to make too much noise, Eirlys shunted back her canvas chair and began clearing up. The light was fading fast now, and she lit the lantern she used of an evening when she didn't want to go inside. It cast a gentle glow on the small picnic area. This was her favourite part of the day, and she didn't know if she could give it all up to go and live in Finn's Forest.

There was Miranda to consider too. How long would her makeover last? Could Hugo be trusted not to turn back into the brat he had been before his accident? Philip had promised to be more hands-on, but he was an international businessman. There would be calls on his time. He wouldn't always be there to pick up the pieces should things fall apart.

Finn shifted in his seat. His head fell forward and he began to snore. It was a sound Eirlys hadn't heard since the days of her marriage to Marcus. She had been on her own for so long now, she wasn't sure she could readapt to being part of a relationship. She had stopped Finn from saying too much because it was a step she didn't want to take — yet.

She had been on one or two casual dates over the past few years but nothing very meaningful. There had been Gareth to consider, and of course Martha. She was another stumbling block to any proposed change. Camp life wouldn't be suitable for a lady of her years. Although it was a big wrench for her, she had moved from Cornwall to be with the family, and was now settled in her bungalow. Eirlys was reluctant to subject her to more disruption.

The sound of a vehicle bumping over the rutted field interrupted her thoughts. Jack was doing his last-minute circuit, making sure all the cows had been rounded up.

Eirlys strolled over to speak to him. He touched the peak of his cap and turned off his engine. 'Quite a bit of coming and going this evening, I see.' He nodded towards her caravan.

'I hope you don't mind,' Eirlys replied.

'As long as the animals aren't disturbed and the gates stay shut, I don't mind at all. What's it all about?' he asked in his direct manner.

'Finn Hart.' Eirlys gestured to where he was still sleeping peacefully.

'That the new man, is it?'

Eirlys was glad Jack couldn't see the flush of colour flooding her face. 'He runs Finn's Forest.'

'I thought you were staying away longer. Didn't you like it?'

Eirlys skirted round the full story. 'There were issues.'

Jack restarted his engine. 'I won't ask any more questions. But if you want my opinion, your Finn looks a good sort.'

With a cheery wave, Jack departed. A

'good sort' was the closest Jack would come to saying he approved of someone. She wondered what he would make of Philip and Miranda Hargreaves. Were they good sorts too?

With a sigh, Eirlys made her way back to the caravan. 'Finn?' she shook him gently by the shoulder.

He stirred, opened his eyes and frowned at her.

'You fell asleep,' she said. 'I didn't like to wake you, but it's getting late and you've got a long drive back. Unless . . . ' She hesitated.

'Unless what?'

'You could sleep over. There's not enough room in the caravan,' she added hastily, 'but you could bed down out here. It's a warm night and I've plenty of rugs.'

'I wouldn't want to impose.'

'You do stand the risk of being woken up by a herd of cows in the morning. They've already had a go at poor old Philip. They love visitors, so there's no chance they'll leave you alone.'

'What about you?' he asked.

'Are you asking me if I'll leave you alone?' She tried to turn his remark into a joke.

'I meant, would you mind if I slept over? Would the farmer object?'

'He thinks you're a good sort.'

'When did he say that?'

'Just now, when you were snoring your heart out.'

'I do not snore,' he insisted.

'Yes you do,' she teased, 'but I don't think I'd better let the gang at the camp in on that one, or they might get the wrong idea. If you're going to stay, I do have a bottle of unopened wine we could share.'

'Why don't you fetch the wine,' Finn suggested, 'while I park my vehicle away from any inquisitive cows?'

Not sure if she had made the wisest of moves, Eirlys did as she was bid. Perhaps her days of behaving sensibly were over, she thought as she bent down to retrieve the bottle of wine from under her bunk.

14

Martha Pendragon was the last person in the world anyone would have cast as a fisherman's wife. She was small and plump, and loved perfume, nail varnish and her weekly trip to the hairdresser. Her clothes would be classed as elegant casual, and her greatest delight had been when she had passed her driving test on her fiftieth birthday and treated herself to a car. On sunny days she could be seen driving through town in her open-topped vehicle, waving to all her friends and acquaintances before remembering just in time to pull up at red lights.

'I did find the written part taxing,' she had confided to Eirlys after she'd passed. 'It's been years since I've sat an exam. Everyone else was so young.'

'I don't think you should reapply your lipstick while you're at the wheel,'

Eirlys now cautioned her mother-in-law as she sat beside her in the passenger seat.

'Nonsense. These road works take ages to get through. We won't be moving for hours yet. Now tell me what that handsome young man was doing in a four-track outside your caravan this morning. I've never seen anyone swerve out of my way so fast. I'm sure I saw the whites of his eyes.'

'That's because he thought you weren't going to stop, Martha,' Eirlys explained patiently. It was a conversation they often had, and nothing Eirlys said would convince Martha that she could be in the wrong when it came to her driving skills.

'I've got a clean licence, I'll have you know.'

Eirlys loved Martha to bits but she wasn't blind to her faults.

'I'm a lot safer in my car than you are on that rackety old bicycle of yours.'

'Let's not go there, Martha,' Eirlys pleaded. Her head was slow to clear this morning, and she wasn't sure she was up to a one-to-one with her mother-in-law.

'So, what gives?' Martha demanded as they eased forward in the queue. 'Was the elusive male the infamous Finn Hart?' Eirlys nodded. 'Thought so. I've heard quite a bit about him.' She cast her daughter-in-law a speculative look. 'My contacts tell me he's going places. And talking of going places, wasn't it rather early in the day to come calling?'

Eirlys blocked Martha's line of enquiry. 'No earlier than you.'

'I'm family. Come on, fess up.'

'We sat up late talking last night and had a glass or two of wine, and we both overslept this morning. He had to get back to the camp — Finn's Forest — that's why he left in such a hurry.'

'I see.' Martha managed to inject a wealth of meaning into the two words.

'He slept under the canopy.' Eirlys didn't like to have to justify her actions, but Martha did deserve an explanation.

'Your personal life is your own affair, darling, but when he didn't hang around to be introduced it did cross my mind that the poor man was running for cover.'

Eirlys smiled. 'I will admit I told him you could be prickly.'

'Did you add that I don't suffer fools gladly?'

'I think he got the picture.'

'Hm.' Martha tapped her steering wheel with an elegantly manicured fingernail. 'We do need to talk, and there's no time like the present.'

'Where's Gareth?' Eirlys ventured to ask. When she'd seen her mother-in-law roaring through Jack's gates earlier that morning, she'd hoped they weren't in for a showdown. Finn was already preparing to leave, and Eirlys was glad that due to pressure of time he'd opted for the safe choice of giving Martha a wide berth. If she should be in one of her rare frosty moods, his journey could have been seriously delayed.

'He's off telling his friends all about

Finn's Forest. The lady in the library has given over the children's section to the discovery of outdoor activities, so he's the star of the show. They've got hands-on staff looking after things. I'm not due to pick him up until four o'clock this afternoon, so we've got all day to thrash things out.' She put her foot down as the green light came into sight.

'I don't know where to start,' Eirlys admitted.

'I'd say Finn Hart might be a good place.'

'It's a long story.'

'And I've had a garbled version of events from Gareth. As far as I can gather, my grandson is in charge of something called a mud slide. His new best friend is called Archie. He thinks Hugo might be elected to join their select group, but he's not sure about that one. You'll marry Finn, and everyone is going to live happily ever after. Did I miss anything?'

Eirlys gulped. Clearly it had been a

mistake to leave her son with his grandmother before she'd had a chance to put her version of events.

'I'm a bit confused about Miranda and a dog called Polly,' Martha was speaking again, 'and why you fell out with Finn and came home early, but no doubt you'll put me right on these minor details. When's the wedding?'

Eirlys began to grow annoyed. 'For goodness sake, Martha, that's not how it is at all.'

'I know that, darling,' she said in a softer voice, 'but I wanted to see you smile again. You know you haven't done much of it over the past few years, and you mustn't think I would dream of standing in your way if you wanted to form a new relationship. For my part, I'd be delighted to have more grand-children to spoil, although I wouldn't be their official grandmother. But I hope you won't let a minor technicality stand in the way of things.'

'You'll always be my children's grandmother,' Eirlys reassured her.

'I'm pleased to hear it. Let's have some music and save the other stuff 'til we get home.'

Martha flicked a switch on the dashboard, and any further conversation was drowned out by Martha's beloved play list that as usual was looped to her favourite musical.

With Martha belting out the finale, they arrived at the bungalow. Eirlys was pleased to have the opportunity to stretch her legs. She needed to get her head together, and her insides needed to calm down too. Martha wasn't the slowest of drivers and Eirlys' insides, physical and emotional, were in turmoil.

'Let's have brunch in the garden.' Martha pushed open the front door. 'I didn't have time for breakfast, and I don't think you did either.'

'Good idea,' Eirlys agreed.

Martha's neat little garden reflected her personality. A man came in to cut the grass once a fortnight. The flower-beds were given over to bedding plants that required minimal supervision. A small shed in a far corner housed weeding essentials, and after an afternoon's activities Martha enjoyed spending an hour or two on her patio watching the sun go down, often with one of her many friends.

'Here we are.' She emerged with a loaded tray after having refused any offers of help in the kitchen. 'Scrambled eggs, fluffed up exactly how you like them; toast, orange juice, a pot of tea; and we'll finish up with a slice of jam sponge. I entertained my ladies' group to tea yesterday and it didn't all get eaten, so tuck in.'

★　★　★

'That was delicious.' Eirlys dabbed at the cake crumbs on her plate with her finger and licked them off.

'I'd like to say I baked it, but I didn't,' Martha confessed. 'All my sponges sag in the middle, so I buy them in from a lovely local patisserie.' She leaned back in her wooden garden seat. 'Now, down to business. Who was the man in the smart car who gave you and Gareth a lift home yesterday?'

'Philip Hargreaves.'

'Was that his name? You have a habit of not introducing me to the men in your life.'

'He's Miranda's husband.'

'Ah, now things are beginning to become clearer.'

'He's the main backer of Finn's Forest.'

'Am I correct in assuming that Finn doesn't want to upset him for obvious reasons, likewise his wife Miranda?' Eirlys nodded. 'Is there anything else about this Miranda that I should know?'

'She's Hugo's mother.'

'Wasn't he the boy you rescued?' Eirlys nodded. 'I get the feeling if ever I met young Hugo, I might be telling him a few home truths.'

'His mother does spoil him.'

'There's spoiling and spoiling. Is he a brat?'

'There was a mix-up over some missing trainers.'

'He blamed Gareth, didn't he?' As usual, there was no fooling Martha. 'And Finn stuck up for Miranda and Hugo?'

'Philip, her husband, understands the situation,' Eirlys said by way of explanation.

'When you entered your little competition, I had no idea you'd stir up such a hornet's nest,' Martha remarked.

'Neither did I.' Eirlys sipped some tea to ease the dryness of her throat.

'There's more drama here than any daytime soap.'

'I wouldn't go that far,' Eirlys replied, but Martha didn't appear to be listening.

'You know I only have your and Gareth's best interests at heart, don't you?' She looked unnaturally serious.

'You've always been there for us,' Eirlys replied, 'but please don't do anything outlandish on my behalf. I'll sort things out.'

'What I'm about to say might come as a bit of a shock.'

'I think I know what's on your mind,'

Eirlys pre-empted her.

'No, you don't.'

Eirlys stiffened at the tone of Martha's voice.

'Sorry to be sharp with you, darling, but you really can have no idea of what I'm about to tell you.' She refilled her favourite mug with another cup of tea and fiddled around with the handle of the milk jug as if uncertain how to continue.

'You're not ill, are you?' Eirlys leaned forward and took a good look at Martha. Her eyes were bright and her complexion looked natural.

'As you know,' she eventually began, 'after I was widowed, Marcus was my life. Then it was you, and of course Gareth.'

'I hope you're not trying to say we relied on you too much.'

'Far from it. Family has always been the heart of my life and it always will be. That's why I was so surprised when it happened.'

'When what happened?' Eirlys was

now more mystified than ever.

'The reason why I wanted to see you today. I sense your life is coming to a crossroads, as is mine.'

'I still have no idea what you're talking about, Martha.'

'I suppose I'm talking about a need to return to my roots.'

'Cornwall?'

'I want to move back.'

'Why?'

'Do you remember Jem?'

'Lobster Pot Jem?'

'Did you know he got that name because he lost all his pots one night in a storm?'

Eirlys clenched her fists, biting down the urge to snap at Martha. 'What about him?'

Martha's cheeks were now rather pink as she made a great fuss of stirring her tea. 'Would you believe he's been in touch?'

'From Cornwall? It's miles away. As far as I can remember, he rarely left his village.'

'Via a computer link. One of his grandsons set him up nicely and he sent me a test email. He had my address from a Christmas card I sent him. Anyway, I responded, and now we talk regularly. It started off as something to do on Sunday afternoons. Then we sort of began contacting each other during the week. He's widowed as well. I knew his wife and we chat about the old days, and I began to realise how much I miss the fishing community.'

'I thought you were settled here.'

'I was. I still am. But . . . ' Martha paused. 'If I don't make the change now, then I fear I never will.'

'You really want to go back?'

'Only with your approval. I know it would mean a tremendous lifestyle change for you and Gareth, but from what he's been telling me, things are about to change in that direction anyway.'

'I'm not sure what my son's been saying, Martha, but I'm not about to get married to Finn Hart.'

'Then he hasn't offered you a

position at the camp?' She sounded disappointed.

'Well, yes, sort of,' Eirlys conceded.

'And you turned him down?'

'Not in so many words. I was going to discuss things with you. If I accepted his offer it would mean a new school for Gareth and a complete change of lifestyle for me.'

'Sometimes it's good to go for change, isn't it? And bother the consequences?' Martha queried.

'You've already made up your mind, haven't you?'

'Jem has asked me to marry him,' Martha admitted. 'He knows the setup here and says he'll understand if I turn him down.'

'Do you want to get married again?'

Martha seemed reluctant to look Eirlys in the eye. 'I know I sound silly, but I do get lonely at times. I've got loads of friends and I'm always busy, but there's never anyone to do nothing with on lazy afternoons. Am I making sense?'

'Perfect sense,' Eirlys reassured her.

'Jem and I go way back. My brothers went to school with him, so it's not as if we met last week on an internet dating site.'

Eirlys leaned forward. 'Martha, you mustn't let me stand in your way. Go for it. You have my blessing.'

'I won't do anything immediately,' Martha said with a shaky smile. 'It'll take some time to sort everything out. Would you like to speak to Jem?'

'Now?'

'Why not? Let's go have a chat and tell him the news.'

15

Finn's hug threatened to crush the breath out of Eirlys' lungs.

'I wasn't sure you'd come back.' His voice was a hoarse rasp in her ear as he wrapped his arms around her body.

'This is only a trial run.' His jacket, which still carried the aroma of old bonfire and wet leaves, muffled Eirlys' reply.

'I don't care what it is — you're here and that's all that counts.'

'Finn, please,' she begged. 'I can't breathe.'

'Sorry.' He released his hold and his eyes scanned her face. 'You look tired.'

'I've been busy. There was so much to do, what with Gareth breaking up from school and Martha making plans, then unmaking them five minutes later.'

'The fearsome Martha.' Finn pulled

a face. 'I hope she doesn't think badly of me.'

'Thank your lucky stars that for the moment she has other things on her mind.'

'About that night we spent together — ' he began.

'Lower your voice.' Eirlys cast an anxious glance over her shoulder. 'Trees have ears, and we did not spend the night together. You were outside under the stars and I was tucked up in my bunk bed.'

'Martha isn't making a fuss, is she?'

'Like I said, she has other things on her mind.'

'Thank goodness for that.'

It had been five weeks since her last visit to Finn's Forest, and Eirlys' feet had hardly touched the ground. Martha had been full of plans for her future with Jem, and Eirlys had rearranged her painting schedule countless times, and made endless itemised lists of things to do that still had only been partially completed.

'I wasn't sure what day you were coming. Why didn't you call? I could have come to fetch you.'

'Your wretched rule about no mobiles on site,' Eirlys complained, 'makes you extremely difficult to get hold of.'

'Let's not start on all that again.' Finn held up his hands in mock defeat. 'How did you and Gareth get up here, anyway? I presume you didn't bicycle all the way?'

'Brian Jackson drove me.'

'Why does that name seem familiar?' Finn frowned.

'He's the father of the little girl whose picture I painted.'

'He's still in touch, is he?' Finn asked in an ultra-casual voice.

Eirlys poked Finn in the chest. 'He's a good business contact. He knows loads of people. And what's more, he wants his daughter Jenny to be your first female customer.'

'Hold on, slow down. Nothing's definite yet on that score.'

'She's already registered for the open

216

day, and her classmates are clamouring to join her. You can't afford to turn down good business.'

'Wait a moment.'

'There he is now.' Eirlys waved at the man walking towards them. 'Brian, this is Finn Hart.'

The two men shook hands.

'I think the idea of introducing the girls is a wonderful plan.' Brian was all enthusiasm. 'If Jenny could spend a few days here, I would be a hero in her eyes.'

'You already are,' Eirlys said.

'Kind of you to say so.'

Finn didn't join in their laughter. 'It'll mean a lot of work, so there's no need to get too excited.'

'Have I created a problem?' Brian asked with an anxious frown. 'I've been putting the word round my various contacts and it's generated a lot of interest.'

'So Eirlys has been telling me.'

'If you need any help,' Brian offered, 'I'm quite handy with a hammer.'

'I shouldn't hang about,' Eirlys said, refusing to be intimated by Finn's glare. 'We might take you at your word.'

'Then I'd best be getting back.' Brian looked at his watch. 'But I meant what I said — let me know if there's anything I can do to help regarding the open day.'

'Tell lots more people about it,' Eirlys urged.

'That I promise.'

'Thanks for the lift, Brian.'

'No problem.'

Eirlys turned back to Finn. 'Right, where do we start?'

They were standing in the middle of the compound and were forced to move out of the way as helpers brushed past them carrying various bits of equipment, and staggering under the weight of all the other detritus of daily camp life.

'Can't talk here. The office?' Finn ducked as he narrowly avoided colliding with a huge plank being carried by two burly men Eirlys hadn't seen before.

'Who are they?' she hissed.

'We're revamping the obstacle course.'

'The plan is for the inspectors to mingle with the visitors, isn't it?' Eirlys asked.

'That's the general idea.' He began hunting through the paperwork on his desk. 'I wish Miranda was here.'

Eirlys stiffened at the mention of her name. 'Is there anything I can do to help?'

'Only if you can lay your hands on the latest set of promotional photos.'

'Is this what you're looking for?' Eirlys held up a glossy folder.

'Brilliant.' Finn grabbed the file. 'What do you think?'

Eirlys glanced through them.

'They're good, but . . . ' She paused.

'Go on. I desperately need feedback.'

'They're all posed.' She looked at the pictures of the staff standing around with self-conscious smiles on their faces.

'That's the idea, isn't it?'

'Wouldn't it be better for everyone to take casual pictures throughout a normal working day?'

'You mean steal up on people and frighten the life out of them with a flash gun?'

'That's not what I meant at all,' Eirlys insisted.

'What, then?'

'One of the rangers could take a photo, say of the men with the planks and you ducking for cover, or Archie giggling on the mud slide, Hannah stirring a huge pot of porridge — everyday activities like that. Obviously we'd have to get personal permission from the subjects before we displayed the snapshots, but I don't foresee any problems.'

'And where exactly did you envisage displaying these snapshots?'

'I don't know. On a corkboard, say? I think the display would create a focus of interest and certainly break the ice. We could offer a prize for the best one.'

'You could have something. I'm thinking obstacle course here,' Finn mused.

'Exactly. Everyone's gone headfirst

into the water ditch at some time or another. As long as the subject doesn't create a fuss, it would be a great selling point.'

'It's a good idea, but I have one reservation.'

'What's that?'

'You tell Miranda her photographic skills will no longer be required and that she's out of a job.' Finn grinned.

Eirlys hastily reassessed the position. 'She can still do the press releases. There's no question of her being out of work.'

'Only kidding. But you should see the expression on your face,' Finn gloated. 'I really got you going, didn't I?'

'Where is Miranda?' Eirlys asked carefully, wishing Finn didn't look quite so handsome when he laughed.

'Sunning herself somewhere warm and sunny with Philip, last I heard.'

'And Hugo?'

'Helping out on site.'

'Why is Archie still here? I thought the cabins were out of commission while the renovations are being carried out.'

'His parents are abroad, so he's staying on as company for Hugo. You won't believe what happened yesterday.'

'Surprise me.' Eirlys couldn't keep the note of apprehension out of her voice.

'The mud slide?'

'Don't tell me. Hugo fell over in it.'

'Archie pushed him into it, face down.'

'What?' Eirlys could see all their recent hard work going out the window. 'How could Archie have been so silly?'

'He insisted it was an accident, but I didn't believe the little imp for one moment. He's as angelic-looking as a choirboy, but he didn't take me in for a second. He had guilt written all over his face.'

'What are we going to do?'

'Nothing. First-hand reports say Hugo took it in good part.'

'Then Archie had better watch his back.'

'Have you seen Hugo yet?' Finn asked. Eirlys shook her head. 'He's a changed boy.'

'In what way?'

'People are beginning to like him.'

Eirlys was still gaping when the door to the office flew open and Gareth raced in.

'Steady on.' The draught of air his arrival created disturbed the mountain of papers on Finn's desk. He anchored everything down as best he could with his arms outstretched. 'Where's the fire?' he demanded.

'It's Archie.' Gareth covered his mouth with his hand, scarcely able to contain his laughter.

'What's happened?' Eirlys asked, maternal instincts on full alert.

'Hugo tied the laces of his trainers together when he was wasn't looking and he's fallen into the water jump. I took a picture. Sorry,' he mumbled with a shamefaced look at Finn, 'it was Mum who broke the rules. She left her phone in the pocket of my jacket.'

Eirlys put a protective arm around her son's shoulders. 'At the risk of being accused of nepotism, I think we have our first corkboard photo.'

* * *

The following days passed in a blur of schedules that were revised, then re-written, then abandoned for something completely different. Everyone worked from dawn to dusk, and the air was constantly filled with the sound of sawing, power drills and the clang of metal.

'We need a VIP to start things off on the big day,' Finn announced over a snatched supper in his office. He and Eirlys had taken to eating together of an evening as it was about the only free time they had during the day.

'Do you know any VIPs?' Eirlys asked.

Finn shook his head. 'Not really my thing. How about you?'

'Me neither.'

'Perhaps Philip Hargreaves could help,' Finn suggested.

'I don't think Philip mixes with the sort of people we're looking for. The youngsters will want someone they can relate to.'

'Well I don't know any celebrity footballers.'

'Dean's got a cousin.'

'I've got one too, but I'm not thinking of asking him to do the honours.'

Eirlys did her best to ignore the twinkle in Finn's eyes. So far their relationship had been purely professional, but the situation was getting more difficult as they were daily thrown into constant contact, sometimes under the most testing of conditions. Throughout all the dramas, Finn had maintained his cheerful sense of humour, and Eirlys began to find it a struggle not to reveal her growing depth of feeling for him.

'We were walking the obstacle course together my first day here,' she said, 'and he told me about him.'

Finn smacked his forehead with the palm of his hand. 'Of course. I'd completely forgotten. His cousin plays for one of the league teams, doesn't he? Dean was boasting about it one night round the campfire until we told him to put a sock in it. I'll get on to it right away.' He scribbled down a quick note. 'There's just one another thing,' he said in a slow voice.

'Yes?' Eirlys looked up from her checklist.

'I was thinking about the zip wire.'

'Yes?'

'We could do a demonstration to explain how it helped you overcome your fear of heights.'

'You want me to do it again in front of a crowd?'

'What if we both do it as a sort of showpiece?'

'How?'

'Harnessed together. I think it would hold great appeal, don't you?'

'Not for me it wouldn't.' The thought of being strapped bodily to Finn was too much.

'I think it's a marvellous idea, Finn,' a voice broke in, 'especially as Hugo informs me you're in the market for natural photos. It would be a marvellous opportunity for lots of snapshots. I've even bought my son a new camera as a present.'

Eirlys spun round to face a suntanned Miranda standing in the doorway. By her side was an equally happy-looking Hugo. The next moment a flash went off, temporarily blinding her.

'My first one for the corkboard,' Hugo announced proudly. 'I'm going to win the prize.'

16

'What if nobody comes tomorrow?' Gareth asked in a fearful voice, pausing from cleaning his teeth to look over his shoulder.

'Granny Marcus has said she will,' Eirlys replied. 'And have you ever known her break a promise?'

'No.' Gareth resumed his vigorous brushing.

Finn had stipulated there were to be no bookings at the camp in the lead-up to the open day, in order to give everyone a chance to clean all areas and to make sure the equipment was in tip-top condition.

Only Gareth and Eirlys had stayed on. Archie's parents had returned and Hugo had gone back home. With plenty of free space, members of staff had flitted to and fro, engaged on last-minute errands and publicity work.

Eirlys had to admit that Miranda had more than proved her worth. She had an excellent network of local contacts, and not a day went by when either Finn or Eirlys didn't take a publicity call in the office.

The corkboard was now covered with slice-of-life photos. From the attention it had received before the open day, it was obvious it was going to be a great success with visitors, who would be invited to vote for their favourite snapshot.

Gareth replaced his brush in the tooth mug. 'I got a good luck card from Archie. Hugo sent one too. They said they'd be here early.'

Eirlys put her arms around her son and hugged him. 'I'm glad you're all friends now.'

Gareth wriggled free from his mother's embrace. 'You're friends with Finn too now, aren't you?'

Eirlys lowered her eyes and picked Gareth's towel up off the floor.

'I'm supposed to do that,' he insisted, tugging it out of her hands. 'We're responsible for our own things,' he quoted Finn's rule.

'Don't forget to hang it on your hook then,' Eirlys reminded him. 'Number seven.'

A special bunk had been made up for Gareth in the guest accommodation as the cabins were decommissioned. The ground floor had been cleared of all its stock and Gareth slept there whilst Eirlys occupied the attic. The staff appeared to accept the situation between Eirlys and Finn as natural, and there had been no adverse comments about her staying on, not even from Miranda.

* * *

'Philip and I had the most glorious time in Portofino,' she confided to Eirlys one afternoon as they'd shared a cup of tea in the kitchen. 'We swam and sunbathed, went for lovely long walks and ate the most delicious food. It was like a second honeymoon, and I have you to thank for it.'

'Me?' Eirlys spilt some tea on the scrubbed pine table.

'Our relationship was growing stale.'

Eirlys wriggled uncomfortably in her chair. Girly chats with Miranda were something new to her and she wasn't sure how to deal with them.

'Finn's a very attractive man and I have to admit I used him.'

'Are you sure you should be telling me this, Miranda?'

'I have to,' she replied. 'You see, I want you to know that all those innuendos and other stuff I came out with weren't really true. I love my husband very much, but with him it was always work. I wanted him to remember he had a family, and I thought if I could make him jealous he might not go away quite so often.'

'Then I'm glad everything worked out for you.' Eirlys gathered up their cups and rinsed them in a bowl of soapy water.

'Hugo's a different boy too, now he has his father's attention. You do like him, don't you? Hugo, I mean.'

'Yes, I do,' Eirlys admitted.

Before he had gone back home, Hugo had proved a useful aid with the various tasks that needed to be completed in time for the inspectors' visit. Being older and taller than Gareth, he was physically able to reach up higher than the younger boy, and his help was invaluable.

'Things changed after his accident,' Miranda explained. 'He began singing your praises and said how much he liked you and that I wasn't to be horrid to you or Gareth anymore. It took my son's advice to make me realise how badly I was behaving to everyone.'

'We really should be getting on.' Eirlys had edged towards the door.

'I want you to know that if you and Finn . . . ' Miranda paused as if uncertain how to go on.

'If we what?' Eirlys prompted.

'The talk round here seems to indicate that you're going to get together.'

'Then the talk round here is wrong,' Eirlys insisted.

Miranda looked unconvinced by her

denial. 'Whatever.' She shrugged her shoulders. 'I only want you to know that it's fine with me. In fact, I would quite like it. It would mean you were both settled and happy.'

* * *

After putting an exhausted Gareth to bed, Eirlys sat alone on her bed. There still wasn't much room to move around, but she hadn't felt like going for her usual night-time walk. Finn had been out all day finalising last-minute details, and she had only caught a brief glimpse of his brown felt hat as he'd driven out of the compound on yet another errand.

What Miranda had said was disturbing. Were people discussing their relationship? She supposed it was only natural. She had stayed on while everyone else had been asked to leave apart from the staff and voluntary helpers. Everyone must have wondered what she was doing here.

Even though her days had been full

and long and she had fallen asleep the moment her head touched the pillow, she suspected someone else could have done her work equally as well; someone like Miranda or Dixie.

She had not seen much of Dixie lately, who had been detailed to oversee the arrangements for the proposed influx of girls registered for the open day. Her workload had increased to such an extent that she had been granted the use of a personal assistant.

As for Finn, Eirlys had managed to keep their relationship detached and on a business level. After the first day when he'd greeted her so warmly, he hadn't mentioned anything about any permanent appointment, and Eirlys had been reluctant to approach the subject again.

She sighed and wished Martha hadn't taken herself off to Cornwall. Although she didn't begrudge her mother-in-law's newfound happiness with Jem, she did miss her company and sensible advice. Talking to Martha always put her problems into perspective. If Eirlys was invited to stay on permanently, the first thing she was going to do, she decided, was to make sure authority figures were allowed to carry mobile phones on them at all times. That way she could always talk to anyone whenever she wanted.

A discreet tap on the door made her jump. 'Who is it?' she called out.

'Me. Finn. Can I come in?'

'Er . . . ' Eirlys looked round the cramped space.

'Actually, it might be better if you came outside,' Finn said. 'There's hardly enough room to swing a cat in here.'

'Be with you in a minute.' Eirlys scrambled off the bed and did a quick inspection of her appearance in the mirror; then, annoyed with herself for succumbing to such vanity, opened her door.

'The campfire's still lit. Fancy sitting by it?' he asked. 'There's coffee on the go, or tea if you prefer. Hannah's left some hot water in the billy can.'

'Tea would be lovely,' Eirlys replied.

She followed him to the fire and watched him fill two mugs. His long, lean fingers were scarred with cuts and bruises, evidence of his recent physical work.

He sat down beside Eirlys on the bench and sipped his tea, a thoughtful expression on his face. Seated beside him, she tensed and waited for him to speak. After a few moments he raised his eyes to hers. 'I'm sorry I haven't been around much recently,' he said.

'We've all been busy,' Eirlys admitted, taut with apprehension, wondering where the conversation was leading.

'How are things going with you?'

'Fine.'

'You haven't been avoiding my company, have you?'

'Why should I do that?' Eirlys demanded.

'I don't know. You've no qualms about the zip wire demonstration?' Finn asked.

Eirlys swallowed a mouthful of tea. She did have qualms about the demonstration, but not the sort she suspected

Finn was referring to. For whatever reason, she had allowed herself to be talked into it, and she wasn't about to back out of the deal.

'If it helps youngsters conquer their fears, then it will be worthwhile,' she replied.

'I'm glad we agree on that,' Finn acknowledged her reply with a smile. 'Dixie tells me the take-up for the open day has exceeded expectations. Your friend Brian Jackson has proved an invaluable asset. He's been putting the word around to all and sundry. We've had a slot on the local radio morning coffee programme — Miranda dealt with that one. Someone's put up flyers just about everywhere you can think of, and the website's in danger of crashing from all the hits.'

'And after the open day?' Eirlys asked in a quiet voice.

'I don't follow you.' Finn frowned.

'Will things go on as before?'

'That depends.'

'On what?'

Finn's eyes glittered in the firelight. 'Are we talking professionally or personally?'

'I'm not sure.' Eirlys began to feel uncomfortably warm from the heat of the fire and the closeness of Finn's body beside hers.

'Professionally, everything hangs on the inspectors' decision. Personally, well, I'm not very good at this sort of thing,' he admitted. 'When you come from an all-male environment, it's not easy to express your feelings. I've got two brothers,' he explained with another half-smile. 'One's a welder in a car body shop and the other's a painter and decorator, both very masculine occupations. There wasn't much time for what my mother would have termed fancy talk when I was growing up.'

'It's the same with the fishing community. They're a tightly knit lot and don't open up easily to anyone.'

Finn nudged a dislodged log back into place with the tip of his boot. He was the first to break into the silence that had fallen between them. 'Have you given any more thought to staying on here full-time?'

Eirlys had thought about little else, but she wasn't going to let on to Finn. 'Perhaps we should talk about it after the open day when the inspectors have made their decision.'

'To help you make your decision, Dixie would be an excellent house matron for the girls, but she doesn't have children,' Finn said.

'I don't have daughters either,' Eirlys pointed out.

'You understand how children work.'

'That's an advantage in an activities camp,' Eirlys acknowledged with a reluctant smile, 'but you make them sound like robots when you talk about how they work. Every child is an individual. There's no one formula.'

'Clearly I have a lot to learn in the parenting department,' Finn teased.

Eirlys felt her colour rise and wished she wasn't seated so close to the fire or Finn. 'Gareth has finished his mud slide,' she changed the subject.

'I'm not sure that suggestion was such a good idea,' Finn responded. 'It's going to be awfully messy.'

'You'll have a lot of happy boys on your hands.'

'But not such happy parents, I think.'

'Mud comes off in the wash,' Eirlys reassured him. 'I just hope not too many girls want to have a go.'

'Surely they won't want to,' Finn protested.

'Brian tells me Jenny is very keen on the idea, but he's not so sure of his wife's take on the situation.'

'When were you in touch with Brian?' Finn asked casually.

'He called by the other day to pick up some more promotional leaflets from the office. No one could find you so I dealt with him.'

'I wish I'd known.'

'Why?'

'I like to keep track of things and I'm not sure I want unauthorised people in the office.'

'He's not a spy,' Eirlys insisted, 'and if you turned your wretched radio thing on occasionally it would stop people wasting their time running round in circles looking for you.'

Finn held up his hands in a gesture of apology. 'You know how I am about technology.'

'I also suspect you feel the same way about Brian Jackson.'

'I'm sorry?' Finn frowned.

'You don't trust either of them.'

'Hang on a minute, I never said anything of the sort.'

'You didn't have to. I can tell by the way you talk about him.'

'He does seem to enjoy your company, I must admit.'

'The same way you enjoy Miranda's?'

'That's an unfair remark.'

'Is it?'

'Miranda and I are just good friends.'

'It looked more than that the day Gareth and I arrived.' Eirlys stood up. 'I'm tired,' she announced, 'so if you've said all you've wanted to say about

Brian and me, I'm going to call it a day.'

'Eirlys,' Finn called after her. She didn't turn round. She was too annoyed, and she feared if she did she might very well tell Finn Hart exactly what she thought of his double standards.

17

Eirlys did not think she would ever forget the sorry spectacle of a sodden Miranda clambering out of the wet ditch. Her expensive hairdo was reduced to rats' tails that looked almost as angry as the expression on her face. Gareth, Archie and Hugo, as supporting spectators, hardly helped the situation by collapsing with laughter.

'Can't help you out, Mum,' Hugo trilled. 'It's a tradition. You've got to do it yourself.'

'You pushed me.' Miranda shook her hair out of her eyes. The expression on her face reminded Eirlys of a bulldog who had been robbed of his precious bone and was bent on tracking down the culprit.

'Chill, Mum.'

'We needed someone to demonstrate how to get out of the ditch,' Archie piped up, 'and Hugo said you'd volunteered.'

'I did no such thing.'

A flashgun chose that moment to temporarily blind Miranda. 'Another one for the corkboard.'

'You can't print that picture,' she howled into the face of the grinning photographer.

'Go on, Mrs Hargreaves,' he coaxed, 'be a sport. It'll do wonders for your local image.'

'It might win.' Hugo was now incandescent with delight.

The boys high-fived in excitement at the prospect of winning the brand-new football donated by Dean's cousin and signed by his team. When a howl of outrage went up from Dixie and Eirlys that the last thing they needed was a football, Finn agreed to donate a bicycle should the winner be female.

'Sounds like he hopes you're going to win,' Dixie gumshoed out the side of her mouth as Finn made his announcement.

Eirlys flushed. She agreed with Dixie. Finn didn't have to be quite so obvious in his choice of prize. Everyone knew she possessed a bicycle that was on its last legs.

A loud cheer went up following Miranda's emergence from the wet ditch.

'I thought Miranda was a dragon,' Martha murmured in Eirlys' ear.

'She's had a makeover.' Eirlys watched Hugo hug his mother, whose loss of dignity seemed to have suffered no long-standing after-effects.

The day was turning into one of surprises for Eirlys. True to her promise, Martha had turned up, accompanied by a ruddy-faced Jem.

'How on earth did you manage to entice him away from Cornwall?' Eirlys demanded.

'My fisherman is a useful asset to have around the place for moving furniture and mending just about anything that's broken. And before I finally sell up there are a few things that need doing.' She nodded to where Jem had shuffled off towards the forest. Once Finn's rangers realised he knew how to tie fisherman's knots that no one would be able to undo, they pounced on him, and his skills had been in constant demand.

'Then it's definite?' Eirlys asked. 'You're making the move permanent?'

'You seem to have sorted things out with Finn.' Martha narrowed her eyes. 'Or have you?'

'Not as such,' Eirlys insisted.

'Word of advice?' Martha asked, 'I know now isn't the time or the place, but we may not have much opportunity to talk later.'

'Go on,' Eirlys urged.

'In my book, Finn Hart's the man I would have chosen to replace my son in your affections.' Eirlys blinked. 'Don't worry, darling, I'm not going to stand in your way. I might have done had you chosen a wrong 'un, but you haven't. I want you to be happy, and I know you'll be in a safe pair of hands with Finn.'

'There are issues,' Eirlys began.

'Poppycock.' Martha dismissed Eirlys'

concern with an airy wave of her hand. 'Issues work themselves out. What matters are the serious things in life. Finn works hard. Gareth likes him. What's more, the man is crazy about you.'

'How can you know that?'

'I've seen the way he looks at you.'

'You only met him for the first time today.'

'You mean apart from the time we nearly had a head-on in Jack's field?'

'You can hardly have formed an opinion of him from that encounter.'

'You're absolutely right, of course, but today I liked what I saw. If you're looking for fancy dining or bunches of flowers and sweet words in the moonlight, then, my girl, you are going to be unlucky. But if you let Finn Hart slip through your fingers, I may never speak to you again. Right, subject closed. Where's that grandson of mine? I've heard rumours about a mud slide.'

'You're not thinking of having a go?' a horrified Eirlys demanded.

'Depends how slippery it is.' Martha

winked. 'Only joking. I'm still trying to persuade Jem that I know how to do grown-up,' she sighed, 'but it isn't easy. You know he treats me like cut glass. I love being waited on hand and foot as much as the next girl, but occasionally I have to let my hair down.'

'Then he's still got stars in his eyes?'

'And some.'

'Want me to put him right for you?' Eirlys teased. 'I could tell him what you're really like.'

'Don't you dare.'

'Look out,' Eirlys warned Martha as a stray football soared out of nowhere and came straight towards them.

'Mine,' Martha insisted and ran forward. The next moment she'd delivered a hefty kick and it winged its way back towards the group of boys clustered round a makeshift goal.

'Thanks,' they chorused, looking round anxiously in case someone in authority had spotted their transgression.

'Don't worry,' Martha bellowed, 'it didn't happen.'

'Cheers!' They waved.

'Dean's footballer cousin seems to have inspired them all with enthusiasm,' Eirlys said.

'I must say his wife is a game one, too. Did you see her tucking into that jacket potato cooked by one of the boys? I thought models didn't eat, but she had the works — cheese, coleslaw and mustard, and then went back for seconds. The wretched girl was as thin as a rake.' Martha looked down at her ample proportions.

'Life can be very unfair at times,' Eirlys commiserated.

Martha looked her up and down to a background of the heavy thud of boot against football. 'I hate to ask, but what on earth are you wearing?'

'The latest fashion in zip wire demonstrations.' Eirlys did a twirl. Between them she and Finn had concocted a suitable boiler suit-style outfit with extra padding.

'You're going down the zip wire?' Martha repeated in disbelief.

'Finn talked me into it,' Eirlys admitted.

'And you say you're not in love with him?'

'I'm not.' Eirlys could see Martha wasn't convinced by her denial.

'Rubbish. No one — not me, not Marcus, not even Gareth — has ever been able to persuade you to climb up to the lowest branch of a tree. Finn has got you swinging about the place on wires like a superwoman.'

'We thought it might be a good idea to show the children how I overcame my nerves.'

'Well, I suggest at the same time you overcome your scruples and tell Finn you're in love with him, you're mad about him, and you can't live another day without him.'

'I can't do that.'

'Yes you can, and no more nonsense about Miranda Hargreaves providing any opposition. I caught her embracing a very handsome man, and I have been reliably informed that man is her husband Philip.' Martha straightened her glasses. 'So, as Jem seems to have deserted me, I am off to inspect the mud slide. I'll catch up with you later — if you're not dangling from a tree, that is.'

A group of clipboard-clutching officials passed by. Having insisted on no special treatment, they were doing their best to mingle with the hordes of excited children, and in some cases equally excited parents.

'It's a pity Finn doesn't run a camp for frustrated fathers,' one of the mothers commented to Eirlys, explaining how her disappointed husband was turned away from the obstacle course.

'One step at a time,' Eirlys laughed.

'Our daughters are so looking forward to coming here next summer if Finn gets the go-ahead to expand. I'd better go and see what they're up to. I haven't seen either of them for a while.' The woman bustled away.

Eirlys glanced at her watch. The zip wire demonstration wasn't due to start for at least another hour. She decided it might be a good idea to circulate and see how things were going.

'Yoo hoo.' She turned to see a red-headed woman striding purposefully towards her. 'You're not an easy lady to track down. Cassandra Jackson,' she introduced herself.

'It's nice to meet you,' Eirlys replied.

'Brian's been singing your praises all day. So has my Jenny.'

Eirlys began to feel uncomfortable.

'I can't thank you enough,' Cassandra continued. 'Jenny used to suffer from terrible asthma. We'd taken her to every specialist we could think of, but since she started practising for the three-legged race it's completely cleared up. Then, when she received first prize, she was ecstatic.'

'Excuse me?' Eirlys interrupted.

'You didn't see? That's a shame. Yes, she and Hugo Hargreaves cleaned up. They led the field all the way. He's a nice boy, isn't he? So considerate, and such nice manners. He made a very sweet speech of acceptance, letting Jenny take all the credit.' Cassandra laughed. 'I think my daughter's in love with him.' She inspected her designer watch. 'Goodness, I must dash. Brian wants me to join in the bird's nest hunt. I haven't done such a thing since I was a girl, and that's more years ago than I am prepared to admit to. Nice to meet you.'

Eirlys stifled a shriek as a smelly figure waded towards her like a creature from the swamp. 'I'm going to have to take a shower before we do any zip wire demonstrating,' it said.

'Finn?' Eirlys peered into his light brown eyes, the only part of his face that wasn't covered in mud.

'That wretched son of yours insisted I have first go on that mud slide he and his evil conspirators have constructed. No one told me how slippery it actually was. I lasted two seconds.'

Eirlys was unable to control her laughter. 'I'm sorry I missed it,' she admitted, wiping her eyes.

'I'm glad you find my discomfort so

amusing.' Finn flicked mud off his fingers. 'Miranda tells me Archie and Hugo had her clambering out of the water ditch. Heavens knows what the inspectors are going to think. It's anarchy out there.'

'Cassandra Jackson's impressed, and I've just seen some of the inspectors walk by. They didn't look like they were about to close us down.'

'Well, keep the boys away from them. I don't want any more mishaps.'

'I think you may be too late.'

'What?'

Eirlys nodded to where one of the younger inspectors, clearly a fan of Dean's cousin, had been delegated to stand in goal for an impromptu penalty shootout. Balls were coming at the hapless inspector thick and fast.

'Do something to stop them,' Finn said anxiously.

'Why? Everyone's having a whale of a time. In fact, I might just join in.'

With a gesture of resignation, Finn headed towards the shower cubicles.

'Don't forget to hang your towel up nicely when you're through,' Eirlys called after him.

Finn spun round so fast Eirlys was forced to take a shocked step backwards. 'Perhaps you'd like to inspect behind my ears when I'm finished to make sure they're clean?'

'Think I'll wait outside,' Eirlys managed to croak.

'You do just that,' Finn agreed with a knowing smile. 'Then we'll show everyone what zip wiring is really about.'

Turning away before her innermost feelings got the better of her, Eirlys walked briskly towards the obstacle course. All around her, excited children regaled their parents with stories of their day's activities. The zip wire demonstration was to be the highlight of the day, after which the inspectors had scheduled a meeting in Finn's office. The weather had been kind to them, for which she was grateful, and only the occasional hiccup had marred the day's activities. But had they done enough to convince the officials that they were fully up to speed?

Hugo raced towards her, a beaming smile on his face. 'Eirlys — I mean, Mrs Pendragon! Everyone's ready for your display. You're not scared, are you?'

Looking into his hopeful face, there was only one answer Eirlys could give him. 'Of course not, Hugo.'

'Good, 'cause I wasn't sure, what with Finn — I mean Mr Hart; we're supposed to call him that today, you know.'

'What about Mr Hart?' Eirlys probed.

'It was his idea to have the platform raised.'

'Raised?'

'Didn't you know? You're going one branch higher than last time. There's Mr Hart now.' Hugo jumped up and down with excitement. 'I'm going to join the penalty shootout. See you later.'

18

'You didn't tell me you'd changed the height of the launch platform,' Eirlys verbally attacked a freshly showered Finn.

'You don't think you can do it?' he challenged, then added in a softer voice, 'You know I wouldn't let anything happen to you. We'll be strapped together.'

His words provided Eirlys with no reassurance. The reminder that his body would be securely strapped against hers was as unnerving as actually doing the zip wire display.

Dean approached, a look of anticipation on his face. 'All ready? Your public are waiting and numbers are swelling.'

'I didn't realise it would be quite such an attraction.' Eirlys looked over to where a group of chattering spectators were gossiping and exchanging details about the day.

'You are the grand finale,' Dean explained.

Eirlys turned back to Finn. 'You didn't tell me that either.'

'Guilty on both counts. Seriously, Eirlys, we have a lot hanging on this one. If you really don't think you can do it, it's not too late to back out.'

Eirlys blinked to clear her vision. It wasn't easy concentrating when she knew so many pairs of eyes were fixed on her and so much was expected from the display.

'Why didn't you suggest a sunrise walk as a finale?'

'We can do that later if you like.' A smile tugged the corner of Finn's mouth. 'I don't suppose any of us will be getting much sleep tonight, so if you want to hug a bouncing bunny or cosy up to a badger or two at sunrise then I'm up for it.'

'Jem's done a fantastic job on the fixtures,' Dean, who hadn't heard the exchange, explained to Eirlys.

'Martha's Jem?' Eirlys repeated in surprise.

'He's very hands-on. Knows his knots. Martha's quite a lady too, isn't she?' Dean chuckled. 'She told him he'd better make sure everything was passed out one hundred percent, as she'd never forgive him if anything went wrong. He's had a look at the new zip wire platform and it passed inspection.'

'There you are then, two of us are on your side,' Finn said. 'Me and Jem.'

'Don't forget Martha.'

'Everyone's on Eirlys' side,' Dean added. 'Your story has provoked a lot of interest.'

'My story?'

'The competition win, and how you overcame your fear of heights and tree-climbing, and what it's done for your self-confidence. It got the highest number of hits on the website.'

'I don't remember saying any of that.'

'Miranda did big up the last bit,' Finn admitted with a shamefaced smile, 'after you reconsidered your decision about helping out with the publicity. But she is on your side too, and Hugo thinks you're great.'

'Much more of this praise and I won't be able to get my safety helmet on,' Eirlys complained. 'My head will be too big.'

'Right then.' Finn adjusted the straps of his harness and looked expectantly at Dean. 'Let's get the show on the road.'

The spectators settled down as Dean performed the introduction. Eirlys was hardly aware of anything that was going on around them. She needed to focus on reaching the higher-level platform without losing her footing or disgracing herself in front of the inspectors. Rangers were straddled across the branches and eager hands reached out to guide her up. Several patted her back and told her to go for it. She could hear Finn breathing behind her and the tree trunk shaking as he changed his foothold.

'Not far to go,' Dixie said, waving down from the highest branch.

Eirlys shaded her eyes against the afternoon sun. 'What are you doing up there?'

'Girl power,' she called down. 'I

couldn't let you do it all on your own.'

Eirlys' harness was beginning to chafe and she wished Finn hadn't insisted she wear so many layers of protective clothing.

'Made it,' Dixie announced as Eirlys swung her legs over the platform edge and hauled herself onto the new construction. She clung onto the supports and tried not to look down. Below them she heard a ragged cheer as Finn joined her and waved to the crowd.

'I feel like a lunar astronaut,' Eirlys confided while Finn was busy attaching her harness to the clips.

'Then let me take you to the stars,' he said.

Before Eirlys had time to reply, the controls were activated; and with Finn's body against hers, they were flying through the air. Her lungs robbed of breath, Eirlys realised Finn's heart was racing as fast as hers. She rested her forehead against the stubble of his chin and surrendered herself to the experience of soaring through the air in the arms of the man she now knew she loved.

Deafened by the applause and besieged by a barrage of flashbulbs as they landed, Eirlys clambered out of her harness. Finn held onto her hand, guiding her through the necessary procedures to disentangle her arms and legs from the padded boiler suit before they took their bows.

A bespectacled female reporter thrust a microphone under her nose. 'A few words for the local radio, Mrs Pendragon — Eirlys?'

She staggered backwards against the firm wall of Finn's chest. 'Knock 'em dead,' he murmured in her ear as he yanked off the woollen hat she'd worn under her safety helmet.

Aware that he was hugging her in front of a radio station reporter, a local television channel camera and nearly everybody on site, Eirlys nodded mutely and prayed she was up to the task of selling Finn's Forest to the listeners.

'I hope,' she began, 'my experience

today will encourage anyone of a nervous disposition that there really is nothing to be worried about. Flying through the air is an immensely liberating experience, and I'd recommend it as stress therapy any day.'

'Especially when you're trapped in the arms of a man like Finn Hart?' The reporter cast a sly glance in his direction.

Eirlys realised she was going to have to think on her feet to save the interview from sinking into territory she had no wish to visit.

'I've never found any man a distraction when I'm concentrating on the task in hand.'

'Attagirl,' Dixie bellowed from her branch as everyone joined in the laughter that greeted Eirlys' remark.

Finn raised his eyebrows in good-humoured acknowledgement of the jibe.

'Terrific stuff, Eirlys.' The reporter leaned forward. 'By the way, you've got bits of branch in your hair.'

'I've got bits of branch everywhere,'

she responded, her reply receiving more loud laughter. 'And after you've done the zip wire, you should see what falls out of your clothing before you go into the shower.'

'A warning I'll bear in mind.' The reporter grinned and turned to the attentive crowd. 'Now, who's next for the zip wire experience?'

'How did I do?' Eirlys asked as she and Finn backed away from the stampede of youngsters eager to try the junior level platform.

'As usual, you were brilliant.'

Eirlys wriggled free of his hold. 'There's no need to hold my hand; I'm fine now I've got my sea legs.'

'As long as you're sure,' Finn countered, not looking in the least chastened by the put-down.

Eirlys brushed leaves off her T-shirt. 'They should really have interviewed you,' she insisted. 'You've had far more experience at that sort of thing.'

'I wouldn't have made half as good a press as you did. To the listeners I'm a hairy man in a hat, desperately in need of a shave.'

'The listeners wouldn't have known that, but they certainly knew about me having half of Finn's Forest in my hair.'

'Why don't we call a truce? There's no need to go on pretending we don't like each other, is there?'

'Darlings, absolutely brilliant.' Miranda held out her arms and air kissed them both. 'I can't come too close to either of you. This jacket is designer, the very latest fashion, and I want to keep it clean for the inspectors. I mean, one of us has to look respectable, wouldn't you say? Are you auditioning for the Birnam Wood scene in *Macbeth*, Eirlys? Sorry,' she said with a look of mock horror, 'I mean the Scottish play. It's bad luck to mention that one by name, isn't it?'

The expression in Miranda's green eyes was a very different one from the past, and Eirlys joined in her laughter. 'While we're on the subject of personal appearance, you didn't look very respectable clambering out of that water ditch,' she retaliated.

'I asked Philip to have strong words with his son about that, but do you know he was as bad as the rest of you? He couldn't stop laughing.' Miranda now looked outraged. 'Thank goodness I had a spare set of clothes in the car. How do I look?'

'Why ask me?' Finn shrugged.

'Because I want you to tell me I look stunning. I'm as nervous as a cat on hot bricks. First impressions are so important, and it's getting near crunch time. Why can't those wretched inspectors get a move on and put us out of our misery?'

Hugo raced towards them, brandishing a brand new football. 'You won first prize, Mum! Your photo got the most votes.'

'A football?' Miranda raised her eyebrows. 'Something I've always wanted.'

'I could change it for the bicycle if you like.' The reluctance of his offer made Eirlys smile.

'I'm sure a football will be much

more useful,' Miranda assured him.

'And the bicycle can stay on site for everyone to use,' Finn added.

'What do we do now?' Eirlys asked Finn. 'The day seems to be winding down.'

Finn looked round. 'Has anyone seen the inspectors?'

The visitors were beginning to drift back to their cars, tugging reluctant children in their wake. Dixie and the other rangers were positioned by the gate leading to the car park and were handing out leaflets from a stack of black bin liners.

'We're in danger of running out of supplies,' she called over.

'Then get everyone's names and addresses,' Miranda replied. 'I'll enter their details on the database.'

Dixie grimaced. 'Any chance of a hand?'

Miranda pretended not to hear.

Eirlys was still tugging leaves and twigs out of her hair. 'I haven't seen any officials for a while. Didn't you mention a meeting this evening?'

'They've promised not to prolong the ordeal any longer than necessary,' Finn replied, 'so I hope they'll be able to let me have their decision today.'

Miranda raised her plucked eyebrows. 'That soon?'

'We've got to know one way or the other. If they're going to close us down, it will be with immediate effect.'

'They won't,' Miranda reassured him, putting a hand on his sleeve and squeezing his arm.

For a moment Eirlys was reminded of the intimate scene she had witnessed on the day of her arrival and wondered if things were really as innocent between them as she had been led to believe.

'Finn,' a male voice interrupted them.

'Philip, darling.' Miranda's face lit up. 'I hope you're the bearer of good news.'

Her husband was clutching a sheaf of papers. 'I've got hundreds of signatures on this petition Brian Jackson and I cobbled together. I don't know if it'll be of any help, but there are some pretty influential names on the list. Hello, Eirlys.' He grinned at her. 'Auditioning for *A Midsummer Night's Dream?*'

'We've already done that joke, darling,' Miranda berated him, 'except it was a different play.'

'What?' Philip looked confused.

'Never mind. Show me your list.'

She ran her eyes down it. 'You and Brian Jackson have been busy. With these names as backers, Finn, they can't close you down. There are some big hitters here.'

'Then don't lose the list.'

'Here they come,' Eirlys gulped as a group of casually dressed officials made their way towards them.

'Gentlemen,' Miranda gushed, 'I hope you've had a good day?'

'Mr Hart?' The senior official addressed Finn. The expression on his face was giving nothing away. 'May we have a word in your office if you're free?'

With a sinking heart, Eirlys watched Finn lead the deputation across the campus.

'Well, we've done all we can.' Miranda squeezed her husband's hand. 'All we can do now is hope for the best.'

19

Inky black water lapped the shores of the lake. Eirlys rested her head on Finn's shoulder, inhaling the cool morning air. 'Look at that,' she murmured as the sky began to soften at the edges, the black of night turning to a deep mauve tinged with orange.

'Here we go.' Finn's lips moved against her hair. 'The greatest show on earth is about to begin.'

Neither of them spoke for several moments until the sky had completed its dawn display. Eirlys shivered.

'Cold?' Finn tightened his arm around her. She shook her head. 'Tired?' She shook her head again. 'You should be. Neither of us slept a wink last night.'

'Sleep was the last thing on my mind,' Eirlys admitted.

'Me too.'

'The authorities really are granting

permission for all the extras?' Eirlys asked for the umpteenth time.

'They really are.'

When Finn had called for everyone to gather around the remains of the campfire, as he had an important announcement to make, she had suspected the worst. Anxious glances had been exchanged. One or two of the newly recruited female rangers were holding hands with the men, suspecting they might all soon be looking for a new job.

The expression on Finn's face was giving nothing away as he waited for everyone to assemble. Philip had taken Hugo and Gareth off for a last go on their mud slide, and to keep them out of the way whilst Finn delivered his news. 'I'll keep an eye on them for you,' he'd said. 'Hugo is begging to sleep over, so Miranda's making up a bunk in the cabin for them.'

Eirlys had seen the inspectors leaving a few moments earlier with serious expressions on their faces. It didn't bode well.

'First of all,' Finn began, 'I would like

to thank everyone for their hard work. Today has been a great success, and I really do appreciate all your efforts. Nothing would have happened without your commitment, and I know each of you has gone the extra mile. I couldn't have asked for a better team.'

A round of applause broke out, then died away, to be replaced by an air of expectance.

'Rather than hear me ramble on, I'm sure most of you want to know exactly what has been decided.' Finn took a deep breath, then broke into a broad smile. 'Well, guys, we are on.'

After a moment's stunned silence while everyone absorbed the news, a whoop loud enough to startle the wood pigeons broke out.

'Not only have the inspectors given the nod to our proposed plans,' Finn continued, raising his voice above the hubbub, 'they have also agreed that we can carry on as we are while the changes are being made, as long as we follow strict guidelines.'

By now no one was really listening to

anything Finn had to say, and with good-natured grace he gave up on his speech and suggested everyone celebrate the good news, as this would be the last chance for some time to chill out. 'Come next week,' he added, 'you'll be too tired to party.'

The sing-along by the fire had continued long into night; and when the celebration showed no signs of flagging, someone began dancing. The call was taken up by the more energetic rangers, and in the end no one was allowed to sit it out.

When Finn had suggested he make good on his promise to show Eirlys the sunrise, she had agreed with more than a little enthusiasm. 'My feet are killing me,' she admitted, 'but every time I stop dancing, a new partner grabs me.'

'Then let's make a break while the going's good.'

Hannah had appeared with a tray of home bakes, and while everyone's attention was diverted Finn and Eirlys slipped away.

'Is sunrise always this beautiful?'

Eirlys murmured as they rested against the trunk of a convenient tree.

'Each season has its magic,' Finn replied. 'I've seen a frosty sky and it matches a midsummer one any day. Then in spring it's more gentle. And autumn, well, that has a different smell.'

'You're sounding quite romantic,' Eirlys laughed.

'Talking of romance,' Finn said quietly, 'there's no better time to discuss our future than at the start of a new day.'

So many things seemed to be changing all at once. She thought back to earlier that day, when Martha had taken her leave of Eirlys and Gareth while Finn was having his meeting with the inspectors. Although Martha didn't do tears, they all sensed it might be a long time before they met up again.

Martha had hugged her fiercely. 'I wouldn't be leaving you if I wasn't sure you'd manage fine without me.'

'What about Gareth?'

'The young adapt. We'll talk on a video link, and he'll always be welcome to visit whenever he wants to come to Cornwall. You needn't think I'm abandoning my grandson, or you.'

'I'll miss you.'

Life without Martha seemed unimaginable, and Eirlys didn't know if she could wing it.

'Finn won't wait forever.' Martha kissed her on the cheek and an awkward Jem shook her by the hand.

Bringing her thoughts back to the present, Eirlys said to Finn, 'Martha thinks I shouldn't let you get away.'

'Your mother-in-law sounds like an eminently sensible woman. So where do we go from here?'

'It would mean big changes,' Eirlys hedged.

'Isn't that what this has all been about? Change?'

'I don't want to give up my painting,' Eirlys insisted.

'I wouldn't dream of stopping you.'

'And there's Gareth. I'm not sure how he feels about things.'

Finn cast Eirlys an old-fashioned look.

'Want to hear a good one?' he queried.

'Go on.'

'We've already had a man-to-man talk.'

Eirlys straightened up. 'You have?'

'He took me to one side and informed me in very grown-up terms that he wouldn't mind if I married you.'

'He said that?'

'He also went on to say he hoped that if we married it would mean he could live in the forest forever, and that being here was about as cool as things could get.'

'This place has worked a miracle on him. He's a changed child since the day we arrived.'

'I'd like to do something similar for other children. That's why I need you here, Eirlys.'

'Is that the only reason?'

'You know it isn't. If you want me to spell it out I will. I can't live without you and I'll do anything within my power to make you stay.'

'As your business partner?'

'As my wife. Will you marry me?'

'Do you really mean it?'

'We've been through all the bad stuff and we're still talking to each other, aren't we?' Eirlys nodded. 'So?' Finn prompted. 'What's your answer?'

'It seems you and Gareth have already sorted things out between you. And you're wrong, you know.'

'About what?' Finn demanded.

'Being a romantic. You're doing just fine.'

As Eirlys raised her lips to Finn's, there was a disturbance in the bushes behind her. Two small figures ran out, laughing and shouting, 'Surprise, surprise,' before Hugo's voice rang out loud and clear: 'Ugh. Gareth, your mother's kissing Finn.'

'That's all right,' Gareth shrugged it off. 'They're getting married. Did you bring your new football?'

'I thought Philip and Miranda made up a bunk for the boys,' Eirlys said.

'Looks like they forgot to use it,' Finn replied. 'I don't think anyone got much sleep last night.'

'Come on, Mum,' Gareth called out, 'you can stand in goal while me and Hugo practise our penalty shootouts. Dean's cousin says we can have a trial at his club if we're good enough when we're older.'

Eirlys drew away from Finn. 'Is it always going to be like this?'

'I don't think it will normally be this peaceful,' Finn replied as another loud shout rent the air, and Dean and several of the other rangers crashed through the trees demanding to join in the impromptu game of football.

'In that case,' Eirlys said in a soft voice, 'before things get totally out of hand, I accept your proposal to be your wife.'

'Great, now come on.' Finn scrambled to his feet.

'Where are we going?' Eirlys demanded.

'Didn't you hear your son? It's your turn to stand in goal.'

A SONG ON THE JUKEBOX

Pat Posner

Polly has fallen head over heels in love with James Dean-lookalike, skiffle-playing Johnny — whom her mum has judged to be completely unsuitable boyfriend material. When Mum sends Polly to live with Gran in an attempt to split them up, Polly is determined to remain true to Johnny. Will Gran, like Mum, forbid her to see him? And what happened in the past to cause the discord between her grandmother and mother? Polly sets out to discover the truth, and the consequences are surprising . . .

THE TOUCH OF THISTLEDOWN

Rebecca Bennett

When Clare, a recently qualified solicitor, meets Neal on the way to her cousin's wedding in Suffolk, his arrogant views on a woman's place in the profession annoy her. Nevertheless, she finds herself reluctantly becoming very attracted to him, despite her involvement with a married partner in the firm where she works. Suffolk and Neal are never far from her life — or her heart; though when one of her clients makes an unexpected, desperate move, Clare finds she is fighting for her life as well as her future happiness.